SEARCHING FOR ELOCK

For Kim — Enjoy

Carl Keyenris

SEARCHING FOR
ELOCK

CARL KEGERREIS

Searching for Elock

Published by Wheatmark®
2030 East Speedway Boulevard, Suite 106
Tucson, Arizona 85719 USA
www.wheatmark.com

ISBN: 978-1-62787-551-6
LCCN: 2017950622

This is a sequel to my first children's book, *Tibby and His Friend's Big Secret*, published by Outskirts Press in 2010. It is available as both a paperback and an ebook at Amazon, BarnesandNoble.com, and other online bookstores through the distributors Ingram and Baker & Taylor. The paperback can also be purchased directly at OutskirtsPress.com/bookstore.

This story, *Searching for Elock,* is fiction. The names of people, places, and all businesses were created through the minds of this author and his two granddaughters. The comic illustrations were created by artist Kerry Ronan. Any similar names of people, places, and businesses are purely coincidental.

CONTENTS

ACKNOWLEDGMENTS

A special thanks to my granddaughter Ashley, who graduated from a public high school in 2015, receiving a scholarship to a university. Ashley created the character Shirley in this story.

A special thanks to my granddaughter Megan, who graduated from a public high school in 2016. She created the characters King Daggerdash and Little Dash in this story.

A special thanks to artist Kerry Ronan, who graduated from a public high school in 2015 and is attending a local college. Kerry created the comic illustrations placed above each chapter title in this book and the comic illustration on this book cover.

A special thanks to my wife, Sandra, who has supported me while writing this story. A special thanks to the reader who has purchased this book. You will be awarded with cartoons, danger, surprises, excitement, and adventure.

LEARNING A NEW LANGUAGE

Starber was whining, barking, and running through the house when the phone rang. Tibby's mom hollered, "Tibby, take Starber outside, please!"

"Okay Mom."

"Tibby, Rex is on the phone!"

Tibby picked up the phone, hearing, "TB, is that you?"

"Rex, what are you trying to say? Rex, slow down; what are you saying? Rex, I'm on my way." Excited, Tibby quickly returned the phone onto the phone hook, hollering, "Mom, Starber and I are going to Rex's house. Come on, Starber!"

As Tibby arrived at Rex's house, he leaped from his bike and ran toward the huge old walnut tree that supported their tree house. Starber ran toward Rex, barking.

Rex pointed, trembling. "TB, there's a fire. Someone is trying to burn down our tree house."

Tibby hollered, "Rex, quick! Get the hose! Who's doing this?"

Rex grabbed the hose and gave it to Tibby, who ran toward a pile of brush mixed with newspapers and cardboard that was burning and smoking. Starber backed away, growling.

Tibby sprayed the water at the fire, at all the tree branches above, and the tree house. Satisfied that the fire was now out, the boys used shovels from the garage to cover the smoking parts with mud.

Rex shook his head. "Boy, TB, I'm glad I found this before Dad and Mom got home. We wouldn't be allowed in our tree house anymore. I don't know how the brush, cardboard, and papers got there."

Starber pawed at the covered debris and barked. Rex snickered. "TB, Starber is telling us everything is okay."

Tibby, eleven, was tall and thin with short red hair and

glasses. Rex also wore glasses. He was ten, the same size as Tibby, and wore a baseball cap reversed on his head.

The boys climbed the walnut tree ladder and disappeared through their tree house door. Starber stayed below, locating his favorite spot in front of the walnut tree, and lay down. Then he jumped up suddenly and started growling and barking.

Splat! Splat!

Mud balls were hitting the tree house. Tibby grabbed Rex and they lay on the floor as several mud balls flew through the open tree house window and hit the wall behind them. Starber yelped from below as a mud ball hit him while he was chasing someone. Tibby slowly crawled to the tree house window, raised his head, and looked outside. He could see Starber walking back toward the tree. His fur was muddy and he was whimpering.

"TB, what's going on?" Rex asked. "Look at the mud balls stuck on the wall."

Tibby grabbed Rex, hollering "Come on, Rex; I have to check Starber. Someone hit him with a mud ball and he's whining!"

Rex was trembling, and Tibby whispered, "Hey, Rex, it's okay."

"TB, first someone tried to set fire to our tree house, then they threw mud balls at us and hit Starber! Who would do that?"

Tibby replied, "I don't know, Rex, but maybe our friend Fogel will know and tell us what we can do."

The boys climbed down the tree house ladder, and Tibby began examining Starber. He pulled off some mud that was clinging to Starber's fur, and Starber licked Tibby, indicating he was okay. Then Tibby took the hose, washed Starber, and attempted to wash the mud balls off the outside of the tree house. Disgusted, Tibby shook his head and pointed at the muddy mess created by the spraying water. Tibby and Rex climbed back up the tree house ladder and looked at the mud balls stuck on the inside wall.

"Wait till Fogel sees this," Tibby said.

Rex snickered. "You know what, TB? This has been a crazy summer. You had a crazy dream about an Elock, a weird creature who travels in a machine that looks like a brown bean, who was hiding in a mansion. I go with you on your paper route the next morning to the mansion to see this creature. The mansion door opens, Starber runs inside, and I get scared and leave you. You meet a Darnell and Coley Morcort. I go with you again, we both meet an Elock, who is still hiding in the mansion, reading the newspaper you delivered, and becomes our friend. Elock scares

Fogel Jarker, who always picked on us, by changing into a huge spider. Fogel would bully us by hitting us, calling us chickens, and daring us to fight, and because of your dream, he wants to be our friend. Fogel now is a great friend. What a crazy dream you had. Then your dream almost comes true when you receive the paper route from our village paperboy, Greg Gruming. You deliver a paper not to a mansion but to an old farmhouse. You are delivering papers, and Starber helps you rescue a Darnell Morcort, who you believe is drowning in the creek. You rescue him, and he tells you he is riding a fish called Roscoe."

Starber, hearing Rex, jumped at the tree, barking.

"See, TB? Starber remembers. Two weeks ago, Fogel goes fishing with us in the creek, when Coley Morcort arrives on the creek bridge, grabs his fishing pole, and lands a small fish. Fogel, embarrassed, leaves us. We leave my dad's fishing poles at the bridge. The next day, you and I go looking for the poles that aren't there. We end up in Morcort's old barn looking for them, and discover a stairway. We go down the stairs and discover a huge cave. We see Darnell and his sister Coley riding something in a huge cave lake. We see a big fish fly up the cave waterfall. We leave the cave and try to leave the barn, but Coley and Darnell are standing by our bikes. We are scared they will find us in their barn. Starber helps us put a hole in the back of the barn. We move some boards, sneak outside, and approach them walking from the creek bridge. Boy, are we surprised that Coley and Darnell are not wet. We both saw them riding something in the cave lake. We hear them call it 'Roscoe.' Boy, talk about surprises. Later we find Darnell on his porch, playing with a toy that he calls Elock, and another toy that resembles a brown bean. You had dreamed about Elock and his brown bean machine. You dreamed about Coley and Darnell Morcort, who are real. It was real and not a dream when you, Fogel, and Starber, with Roscoe's help, rescue Darnell, Coley, and her parents from cave people living in a cave under Morcort's farm. TB, that was real. You dream about an Elock, who is not human, and a Roscoe, who is a big fish that flies, and Darnell tells you he talks! You've got to be kidding me. We learned a huge secret this summer and we can't tell anyone. Anyway, who would believe us?"

Both boys rolled around laughing while Starber jumped at the tree, barking.

"Hey, TB, when the teacher at school wants to know what we have done this summer, do you think we should tell her and our class how your dream almost becomes real and about all our adventures?"

"Yeah, right, Rex. What would I tell them?"

Rex whispered, "TB, it would be something crazy."

Both boys laughed.

Tibby, giggling, raised his hand. "Hey, Rex, give me five!"

Their hands met with a smack, and Starber, Tibby's sandy-white long-haired shepherd dog was again jumping at the tree, barking.

"Hey, TB, look; Starber agrees with us."

Tibby crawled through their tree house door, climbed down the tree ladder, and whispered, "Starber, we have to find Elock. Come on; let's go find him."

Starber agreed, jumping on Tibby. Rex hollered from the tree house. "TB, wait a minute!"

Tibby watched as Rex climbed down the tree ladder, and Starber greeted him with kisses.

Rex walked over to Tibby, raised his hand, and their hands met, locking their fingers together. They chanted, "True friends together, always."

Rex grabbed his bike.

Coley, who was eleven, tall, and thin with light-red hair, was pulling weeds with her mom in the garden when her young brother playing on the porch spotted Tibby, Rex, and Starber crossing the bridge.

Coley's brother Darnell ran toward his sister, hollering, "Coley, your boyfriend, Tibby, is here!"

Coley looked at her mom and threw her gloves on the ground, pleading, "Mom, Tibby can't see me looking like this."

Mrs. Morcort shook her head, smiled, and watched Coley run toward the farmhouse. Both boys dropped their bikes, and Starber was jumping on Darnell. Tibby waived at Mrs. Morcort, asking, "Is Coley here?"

Darnell waved both arms and ran around Tibby, hollering, "Coley has a boyfriend!"

Mrs. Morcort hollered, "Darnell, stop it! Go tell Coley that Tibby, Starber, and Rex are here!"

Darnell ran to the porch and was about to open the door when Coley appeared, and Tibby was amazed, looking at something new. A small brown bundle of fur was running from the porch toward Starber. It was a small brown puppy with white patches. Starber stood still while it jumped on him. Coley leaned down and grabbed the puppy, holding it in her arms.

Tibby reached over Coley's arms and petted the puppy,

who was kicking and nibbling at Coley and wanting to play with Starber.

Darnell whispered, "Coley has a boyfriend."

Tibby lowered his head to hide a smile. He motioned for Coley to put the puppy down beside Starber.

Coley dropped to her knees, explaining, "This is little TJ." Coley looked different. Her her long ponytail had changed to shoulder-length hair, and she was not wearing her glasses. She was smiling, and looking at her, Tibby thought, *Coley looks like her mom, and she is pretty.*

They watched as little TJ chased Starber around the trees. Mrs. Morcort hollered, "Darnell, come over here with me right now!"

Darnell moaned, "Oh, do I have to?"

Coley replied, "Darnell, you heard Mom." Darnell shook his head and slowly walked toward the garden. Coley approached Tibby, again grabbed his hand, and motioned for Rex to join.

Rex held Coley's other hand, looking at her, and Coley whispered, "True friends together, always."

Tibby asked, "Coley, will you teach us the cave people's language?"

Coley shot a look at Tibby that reminded him of his

mom's angry look when he was in trouble. She let go of their hands, looking very concerned, and demanded, "Tibby, why? You're not going back in the cave, are you?"

Tibby lowered his head to hide his face. "Coley, Fogel and I heard them talking when they tossed Darnell in the cave lake. We want to learn so we can talk like them and no one will understand us."

Tibby looked at Rex. "Isn't that right, Rex?"

Rex lowered his head, replying, "Yeah, Coley, we were going to use it for a code to enter our tree house."

Coley smiled, looking at Rex and Tibby, and said something weird. "Uoy dna Rex era gniyl."

Tibby grabbed her hand with both hands, pleading, "What are you saying?"

Coley laughed, whispering, "You and Rex are lying. Tibby, you want to return to the cave. Why?"

Tibby let go of Coley's hand and walked over to his bike. Coley ran after him, hollering, "Tibby, please don't go back in the cave!"

Mrs. Morcort, hearing Coley, approached her, asking, "Coley, what is going on?"

She looked at her mom, attempting to hold back tears. "Mom, Tibby, Rex, and Starber are going back in the cave."

Mrs. Morcort hugged Coley, replying, "Don't you

remember that your dad, Tibby, and Fogel nailed boards over the barn stairway door and placed large rocks over the other entrance? So how would they get back in the cave?"

Coley wiped her eyes, smiling. "Mom, you're right. I forgot they can't get in there." Coley looked at Rex and Starber, who was pawing at little TJ, then grabbed Tibby's hand. "I'm sorry for not believing you."

Mrs. Morcort, shaking her head, returned to the garden, and Darnell ran toward the barn. Coley looked at Tibby and said, "I'm sorry."

Tibby pleaded, "Will you teach us the cave people's language, so we can speak it?"

Coley held Tibby's hand, nodded her head, and motioned for them to follow her under a shaded tree. She commanded, "Let's sit down here."

Starber laid down beside little TJ, placing his head on Coley's leg. Coley petted Starber and TJ, who was kissing her. Coley was speaking weird words. "Starber sevol gnivah sih srae dehctarcs."

Tibby pleaded, "Coley, what are you saying?"

Coley replied, "Starber loves having his ears scratched."

Everyone giggled, Starber barked, TJ whined, and Tibby begged, "Please, Coley, teach us."

Coley pointed toward the house. "Go upstairs, down

the hallway, and enter the last door on the right. I'll join you in a few minutes. I have to talk to Mom and Dad."

Tibby and Rex ran up the stairs and stopped, looking at each other. They were looking down a long, narrow hallway with several doors on the left and right. Tibby shrugged his shoulders, concerned, whispering, "Rex, which door?"

Rex pointed at the first door, when they heard a loud bang. Racing down the steps and out on the porch, they were greeted by Starber and little TJ. They saw Coley waving from the barn and hollering, "It's okay. Dad's working on an old truck that backfired. Go back to the room!"

Tibby and Rex returned to the hallway, opened the first door, and entered. There was a sign on a closet door: Darnell's Room—Girls Not Allowed—Keep Out.

Tibby, disgusted, shook his head, looking at Rex asking. " Which room did Coley tell us?"

Coley stood in the doorway, looking at Tibby and Rex. "Tibby and Rex, didn't I tell you the last door on the right?" Smiling, shaking her head, and motioning toward the hallway, she demanded, "Follow me."

The room was small, the walls and ceilings had large cracks with pieces of plaster hanging, and a small hanging light bulb was covered with cobwebs.

Rex pointed at it, snickering. "Hey, TB, how long would Fogel stay here?"

Tibby looked at the small wood desk with stacked papers. Sitting down on some old red wooden chairs, the boys looked around the room. A white wooden bookcase was next to a dirty window covered by torn blinds. The bookcase, covered with dust and cobwebs, contained an assortment of stacked books and several piles of papers.

Coley whispered, "My grandfather did his research here." Coley pulled out a chalkboard from behind the bookcase, removed some chalk from the desk, and wrote, Evac elpoep evah sa egnarts egaugnal. Tibby and Rex looked confused. Coley continued. "This is the cave people's language. It's easy to learn. Think about our English words and spell each word backward. Add a letter *s* before each single letter. As an example, if you use a single letter, it would be "*sa*". I wrote on this chalkboard, Cave people have a strange language."

Rex giggled,. "It looks and sounds to me like Native Americns talking in the movies."

Tibby and Rex repeated the words, when Mrs. Morcort arrived, announcing, "We are going to have a barbecue this Saturday. Please come, and please bring Fogel, Starber, and your friends. Starber can play with little TJ."

The boys thanked her, and Tibby, noticing the watch on Coley's wrist, asked, "Coley, what time do you have?"

Coley replied, "It's four forty-five."

Tibby hollered, "Rex, ew deen ot og!"

Rex repeated, "Coley, TB says, 'Rex, we need to go.'"

Coley shook her head, smiling. "You're both good students."

Tibby, Rex, and Fogel sat on the floor in the tree house. Fogel, heavy and shorter than Tibby, age eleven, laughed while Tibby and Rex attempted to teach him the cave people's language.

Tibby shouted, "Yeh, Fogel, uoy dluohs evah nees eht redips sbew ni Coley's esuoh!"

Rex rolled over, snickering, and Fogel, shaking his head, asked, "Coley has spiders in her house?"

Tibby raised his hand, hollering, "Fogel, you got it. Give me five." Their hands met, and Rex joined in, locking their fingers and chanting, "True friends together, always."

Tibby shook his head, disgusted, and stood up. "Earlier today, Fogel, someone tried to set fire to our tree house and threw the mud balls that are stuck on the wall above you."

Fogel hollered, "Oh yeah, who did that?" He jumped

up, as the tree house moved, and hollered, "Let's find 'em! I'll break their necks!"

Tibby replied, "Do you know anyone?"

Fogel interrupted. "It's Kurpit Chilling, who loves to play with fire and would throw the mud balls. That's why I didn't like him or his friends. They are always causing trouble. I better not see him or catch him around here."

Tibby spoke, "Guys, we don't know it was Kurpit or his friends, so let's talk about more important stuff. Rex, we need to speak like the cave people. Can we fool them?"

Fogel sat down, and the tree house moved and creaked. Fogel asked, "Hey, guys, ain't we going to use this for our tree house code?"

Rex, not thinking replied, "TB wants to return to the cave to find Elock."

Fogel stood up and looked at them, shaking his head. "Tib, you had two toys we got from the barn and gave them back to Coley's brother. Why do you want to go back to the cave for toys?"

Tibby gave Rex a dirty look and motioned for Fogel to sit down. Tibby told him about his dream, how he believed Elock may be real and a great friend. Looking directly at Fogel, Tibby explained, "Rex and I believe Elock helped us become friends."

Fogel stood up and raised his hand. Tibby and Rex joined him, locking their fingers and chanting, "True friends together, always."

Tibby continued. "Thanks, Rex. I'm glad I told Fogel about Elock. Several weeks ago, Rex and I saw Coley and her brother, Darnell, riding a Roscoe in the cave lake. Remember, Rex? Coley and Darnell were both dry, standing by our bikes. They had to have a fast cave exit. The answer is somewhere in that tunnel. We have to talk to Darnell."

Rex shook his head, moaning, "TB, you are really going back in the cave?"

Tibby smiled, whispering, "Rex and Fogel, you have to come with me."

Fogel hollered, "Hey, guys, I ain't afraid of the cave people. I sure would like to meet this guy you call Elock. He might be creepy, but if he's our friend, I want to see him change into a spider."

Tibby and Rex were laughing, Fogel was shaking his head, and Starber was barking. Fogel asked, "Hey, Tib, what's the plan?"

Tibby replied, "We have to get Darnell to talk. He has to tell us how he and Coley left the cave." Fogel stomped his foot, the tree house moved, and he sat down.

"Hey, Tib, I'll get the little runt to talk."

Tibby whispered, "Fogel, he's a little kid."

Fogel raised his fists. "Tib, I'll get him to tell us."

Rex offered, "Maybe you could get the fish Roscoe to help."

Tibby replied, "We have a barbecue Saturday at Coley's house. We get information from Darnell and go back in the cave to find Darnell's friend Teboy."

Rex hollered, "TB, you got to be kidding me!"

Fogel, looking concerned, chimed in, "Tib, we have to be cave people, with long hair, bare feet, and wearing some kind of hide."

Rex moaned, "TB, how are we going to look like them?"

Tibby replied, "Let me think about it, and we will plan to meet here tomorrow after lunch."

TiBBY'S FAVORiTE COUSiN — SHiRLEY

Tibby's bedroom window faced the garage and was open as a car pulled into their driveway. Starber's barking woke Tibby. Raising up in bed and looking out the window, he saw a light-blue car park and the doors open. A small girl jumped from the car and ran toward the house.

Starber jumped off Tibby's bed, using his nose to open the bedroom door, and raced through the house, barking. "Oh no, no, no," moaned Tibby, watching his cousin , age six, running and hollering.

18

"Oh, Tibby, you're going to be so surprised! Oh yes, you really, really, really, really are!" Tibby's mom had told him at the dinner table. "Tomorrow were going to have a nice surprise."

Tibby now understood why his dad had lowered his head, smiling. Tibby realized that surprise was Shirley, who caused him headaches and upset stomachs and always stayed at his house a week or more. Tibby's mom would remind him, "Tibby, it's a great cousin-bonding time."

Tibby considered it torture, only a million times worse.

He closed the door, crawled back in bed, pulling the covers over his head, and pretended to be asleep. Tibby heard the bedroom door open and his mother whisper, "Shirley, Tibby is still asleep."

The door closed, and Tibby, under the covers, quipped, "Good, yeah, I'm still asleep."

Tibby dreamed about Fogel, Rex, and him laughing and looking at each other, and Starber was barking. Tibby hollered, "Hey, Fogel and Rex, you both look like you belong in a cave—long hair, beards, feed sacks, bare feet, and dirty skin."

Fogel hollered, "Hey, Tib, you should see yourself! How are we going to disguise Starber?"

Tibby looked at Starber, shook his head, and whispered, "I'm sorry, boy, but you have to stay here." Tibby tied Starber to a small tree by the tent. Starber pulled, bit the rope, and sat whining.

Tibby asked, "Rex, are you sure you want to go with us?"

Rex nodded his head, Fogel raised his hand, and the boys locked their fingers, chanting, "True friends together, always."

Tibby and Rex lifted the smaller rocks from the opening, and Fogel moved the heaviest. The boys entered the tunnel, crawling and sliding on their stomachs. They landed on a flat rock, slid down to the floor, and slowly moved between the rocks toward the water. Tibby, Rex, and Fogel covered their heads while bats, screeching and flying toward the opening, hit them. Tibby made a weird screeching noise, calling Roscoe. The boys shined their lights, looking for a huge wave. They stood there waiting while Tibby continued screeching.

Rex whispered, "TB, maybe Roscoe is swimming in the creek and can't hear you. How are we going to get out of this place?" Fogel replied, "Hey guys we can swim and dive under the rocks to reach the cave lake with the waterfall. What do you think? I ain't scared to swim in this water, are you guys?"

Tibby shook his head, and Rex hollered, "You got to be kidding me! TB, you should have talked to Roscoe so he would be here waiting for us. What are we going to do now? I want to go home."

Tibby rolled over in bed, moaning, "Yeah, you're right, Rex."

"Tibby, Tibby, wake up!" shouted Shirley, removing the blanket. Tibby sat up in bed, covered by a sheet and realizing he had been dreaming.

Shirley hollered, "Oh, really, really, goody, you're awake so we can play."

Tibby watched her jump on his bed, sit and hum some song, and swing her legs in the air.

Shirley smiled. "It's boring playing without you, but I'm really, really, really, really glad Starber is here. Starber is a doll, and it was fun painting him."

Tibby heard Starber whining and saw him sitting in the bedroom closet. Tibby hollered, "What have you done?" Starber was covered in pink paint and was wearing a red dress and red nail polish, and his face was covered with black and red makeup.

Tibby felt sick and hollered, "What did you do to Starber?" Collapsing on the bed, propping his arm on the pillow, he weakly asked, "Why did you do that to Starber?"

Starber was whining and moving around like a spinning top, trying to bite the dress. Shirley, wearing coveralls, her long blond hair in pigtails tied in white bow ribbons, continued to jump up and down on the bed, screaming and shouting, "Oh, I just knew you would love what I have done to Starber! I knew you would love it! I love it too! I really, really do. Oh yes, I really love it! Starber remembers me, Tibby. Oh, I really, really knew he would, and really, you do remember me, right?"

Gently Tibby pushed Shirley out of the room, closed the door, got dressed, and pulled the dress off Starber.

Tibby was in his backyard washing Starber with the hose while Shirley ran around them, laughing. Tibby would spray the water at her and count to ten. Tibby's mom had reminded him to be nice to his little cousin, but maybe Tibby's screaming and hollering in her face would be proper payback. Every time Tibby tried to spray her, she hollered a high-pitched squeal. Tibby snickered and thought that Shirley sounded like Coley or Darnell calling Roscoe.

Tibby's mom hollered from the porch. "Tibby, I am taking Shirley and your aunt Brenda shopping! You need to be home at four today, and plan to spend time with Shirley! Shirley, honey, you need to wash up and change clothes."

Tibby watched Shirley skipping and running toward his house, hollering, "I love to shop, oh yes I do, I really, really, really do!"

Tibby grabbed his bike, hollering, "Starber, let's go!"

Arriving in Rex's backyard, Tibby dropped his bike, climbed the walnut tree, and knocked on the tree house door with their special code. Rex opened the door. Tibby crawled inside to find Fogel sitting in the corner eating potato chips.

Fogel handed the sack to Tibby, telling him, "Tib, have some. They are really, really good."

Tibby looked disgusted and lowered his head. Rex asked, "Hey, TB, what's eating you?"

Fogel replied, "Tib, man, I can't believe you don't want any chips. Hey, Tib, did I say something wrong?"

Tibby shook his head, replying, "Just don't use the words *really, really* okay? My little cousin Shirley is at my house, hollering, 'really, really, really,' and decided to decorate Starber with a dress, painting his nails and face, and making him look like a doll while I was asleep. I had to give Starber a bath."

Rex and Fogel rolled over on the floor, laughing and

shaking their heads, and Starber jumped at the walnut tree, barking.

Tibby grabbed some chips. "Fogel, yep, mighty good. Hey, guys, I have been thinking how we can fool the cave people and find Teboy and Elock."

Tibby didn't tell them about his recent dream, where the boys were stranded in the cave without Roscoe to transport them to the waterfall. Tibby continued. "Rex, you have the fishing poles. I have a tent. We tell our parents about Coley's barbecue and that we want to camp out so we can fish in the creek during the weekend. We can talk to Roscoe, who can help us get information from Darnell about Elock if Fogel can't get any information from Darnell."

Fogel whispered, "Hey, guys, I can find out about Elock from that little squirt Darnell."

Tibby whispered, "Okay, Fogel, we are really, really, really counting on you." They all laughed, rolling on the floor, the tree house moved and creaked, and Starber jumped at the tree, barking.

Fogel hollered, "Hey, guys, any big spiders where the cave people live?"

Tibby knowing he would need to be with Shirley, the little tormentor moaned, "I will soon have to go home and play with Shirley, who is a real pain."

Fogel approached Tibby and patted him on the shoulder. "Tib, I know how you feel because I have a little brother who is a real pain."

Tibby, amazed, shouted, "Fogel! That's great. I have an idea."

Rex moaned, "Oh no, please don't tell me were taking them on the campout."

Tibby replied, "No, Rex. Fogel, how old is your brother?"

Fogel shook his head. "A six-year-old pain."

Tibby stood up. "Guys, I've got one problem. Shirley and her mom are visiting us. We may have to cancel the campout unless you Fogel, could bring your little brother to play with Shirley at my house."

Rex hollered, "Great! Maybe we don't have to go back in the cave!"

Tibby was shaking his head and replied, "Rex, we will never know if Elock is real or in the cave unless we go."

Rex asked, "TB, when do we go?"

Tibby and Fogel agreed that Fogel would bring his little brother, Ralphie, to play with Shirley at Tibby's house. Tibby and Fogel would make plans for the campout and about returning to the cave to find Teboy and Elock.

A TEA PARTY AND PAYBACK

Tibby and Starber arrived home and were greeted by Shirley, who had set up toy dishes on the front room floor. Hugging Tibby, she hollered, "Oh, goody, goody, you are back, really, really back, and now we can really, really play, oh yes we can." She released Tibby and jumped toward Starber, who ran away whining.

She pulled Tibby toward the dishes, and while he was attempting to escape, his mom approached them, demanding, "Tibby, you play nice with Shirley."

Shirley's mom, Brenda, peeked around the corner, saying, "Shirley, you be good to Tibby."

Tibby could hear his mom and aunt talking about how nice it was for him to play with Shirley. Tibby looked at the dishes on the floor and thought, *Oh yeah, right*. The little pain was in front of him, demanding, "Tibby, pick up the cup and drink the tea."

Tibby laughed. "Where's the tea?"

Shirley handed him a plate, asking him, "Tibby, would you like a really, really good cookie? Tibby, drink the tea and eat the cookie. You will really, really like them." Shirley jumped up and raced over to the sofa. "I just knew you really would. Don't you love our tea party?"

Tibby looked at the front door, wanting to hear their doorbell announce Fogel and Ralphie. Tibby drank several cups of air, ate invisible cookies from an empty plate, and was getting angry, even though his mom warned him to play nice. He was thinking, *Why aren't Fogel and his brother, Ralphie, here?*

Shirley demanded, "Tibby, you're not drinking your tea and eating more cookies." Starber was sitting in the hallway, whining. "Hey, Shirley, do you want to go to the park to swing and slide?"

Shirley shouted, "Oh, Tibby, thank you! I would really, really love for you to swing me, play on the merry-go-round, teeter-totter, and the slide."

Tibby tried to smile. He grabbed Shirley and took her outside, placing her on his bike handlebars. The bike wobbled, and Shirley screamed, "Oh, Tibby, this is so much fun! It really, really is!"

Starber looked at them, whining. Shirley moved her legs up and down, causing Tibby to lose control and run into the bushes beside their neighbor's driveway. Backing away, he grabbed Shirley and held her, dropping the bike. Placing her on the ground, Tibby demanded, "Shirley, you wait here."

He parked his bike next to the garage and put Starber on the back porch. Returning to the driveway, he saw Shirley running along the street, holding several items in her hand. Tibby caught up to her, grabbed her, and found the neighbor's mail in her hands.

She squealed, shouting, "Oh, Tibby, look what I really, really found."

Tibby grabbed the envelopes, checking the names and address. Holding Shirley with one hand, he placed the envelopes in the correct mailboxes. Tibby shouted, "Shirley, you can't remove people's mail!"

Shirley, shaking, replied, "Oh, Tibby, I'm really, really, really sorry, yes I am."

Tibby held her hand and walked with her toward the park. Walking into the playground, Tibby saw Fogel on the slide, holding a small boy. Tibby approached, asking, "Fogel, why didn't you bring Ralphie to my house?"

Fogel shook his head, pointing at the boy. "Meet Ralphie, my brother. Sorry, Tib, but Dad told me to take him to the park."

Ralphie, with short, curly blond hair, was the same size as Shirley. Shirley followed Ralphie climbing to the top of the slide, and Shirley hollered, "Oh, this is really, really so much fun!" She leaped over Ralphie, and her legs hit him. Ralphie grabbed the steps, about to fall.

Shirley slid down, and Tibby grabbed her, hollering, "Shirley, what are you doing? You hit Ralphie, and he almost fell."

She pulled away from Tibby, shouting, "Ralphie, I'm really, really sorry."

She climbed the ladder and shoved him, and he slid down and landed on the ground. She followed him down the slide, knocked him down, and shouted, "Oh, Ralphie, I'm really, really sorry!" and ran to the ladder.

Ralphie was laughing, running behind Shirley, climbing the ladder, and shouting, "It's my turn to shove you!"

Tibby and Fogel approached the playground's merry-go-round, sat down, and watched their little pains playing. Fogel whispered, "Hey, Tib, what's the plans?"

Tibby moved the merry-go-round fast, hopped on, and replied, "Fogel, I can't do anything until that little pain leaves."

They were twirling around when a Village Police car pulled into the park. The police officer walked toward the playground. He was big with sparkling badges on his shirt and hat. The officer approached Tibby and Fogel. Tibby was nervous while stopping the merry-go-round. Fogel jumped off, ran to the slide, grabbed Ralphie, and raced from the park.

"Were you and a small girl opening mailboxes and removing mail?" the officer demanded, pointing toward the street and looking at Tibby. "A family that lives on that street reported they saw you with a small girl removing mail and walking toward this park. Son, are you with that little girl?"

Tibby nodded his head as the officer asked, "What did you do with the mail?"

Tibby, trembling and moaning, replied, "My little cousin Shirley, playing on the slide, who is six, was opening the mailboxes and removing the mail. I took the mail from her and returned it to the mailboxes. I'm so sorry."

The officer removed his hat, sat down, smiled, and looking at Tibby, whispered, "Let's talk to your little cousin Shirley."

Tibby jumped up and ran toward the slide as Shirley was climbing the ladder. Tibby was smiling and mumbling, "This is great payback for the tea party. The little pain is going to get it now."

Tibby shouted, "Shirley, get down here now!"

Shirley slid down, landing at Tibby's feet, screaming when he grabbed her. Shirley hollered, "I really, really want to slide." Tibby pulled her, and she screamed again, trying to get away. Shirley tried to get loose, but Tibby dragged her to the merry- go-round. The police officer stood up, and she whimpered, "Are you really a policeman?"

The officer nodded his head, asking, "What is your name, honey?"

Tibby held her hand as she tried to hide behind him. He replied, "This is Shirley."

The officer stooped down, smiling. "Honey, were you opening metal boxes along the street and did you remove anything from them?"

Shirley, hanging on to Tibby and trying to hide behind

him, was scared and crying. The police officer looked at Tibby, demanding, "You kids need to come with me. We will need to call your dad and mom."

Tibby nervously replied, "Please, can't we go home?"

The officer put a hand on Tibby's shoulder while Tibby was holding Shirley's hand and motioned for them to follow him walking toward the police car.

Tibby shoved Shirley in the police car back seat inside the prisoner's steel cage. The police officer started the car and began driving from the park when Shirley started bouncing, jumping up and down on the car seat, and shouting, "Oh, Tibby, isn't this really, really fun? Mr. Policeman, would you really, really turn on your siren?"

The police officer laughed, pushed a button, and the siren screamed. Shirley bounced on the seat, hollering, "Oh, Tibby, isn't this really, really wonderful? It really, really, really is so much fun."

Tibby sat with Shirley in the Village Police Office interview room waiting for his dad or mom. Shirley would jump up from the chair, and he would grab her and pull her back to the chair. Tibby, knowing his dad or mom would be unhappy shouted, "Shirley, sit here and be quiet!"

The door opened, and there stood Tibby's mom and Shirley's mom, looking at Tibby and Shirley and shaking their heads. The police officer entered the room, walking by the women. Both women began asking questions.

The police officer explained, "A resident living in your area reported your kids were opening mailboxes and removing their mail."

Tibby's mom, looking angry, approached Tibby and asked, "Tibby Brawlien, is that true?"

Tibby hung his head, nervous and shaking, and Shirley ran to her mom, crying. Shirley whimpered, "I just wanted to see what was in the big metal boxes."

Tibby shook his head and tried to find some words. "Mom, Aunt Brenda, I'm really sorry. I had parked my bike by the garage, was putting Starber on our back porch, and saw Shirley running along the street removing mail from the mailboxes. I took the mail she was holding and returned it to the correct boxes."

Aunt Brenda asked, "Shirley, honey, is that what happened?"

Shirley, grabbing her mom and shaking and crying, replied, "I just really, really wanted to see what was in the metal boxes."

The police officer left the room and returned, announcing, "I'll talk to the resident who called us and explain what happened. I am sure the kids have learned not to open mailboxes. It's okay for you to take them home."

Arriving at the car, Aunt Brenda was angry. "Tibby, this is the way you bond with your cousin. Sis, as soon as we get back to the house, Shirley and I are leaving for home."

Tibby's mom shouted, "Brenda, you can't blame Tibby!"

Tibby was quiet listening to his mom and aunt Brenda arguing. Shirley was bouncing on the back seat and humming.

Tibby watched with Starber from his bedroom window as his aunt Brenda loaded suitcases in her car and placed the seat belt on Shirley. Tibby's mom and aunt were still having words as the car was moving down the driveway.

Tibby hugged Starber, whispering, "Starber, I don't believe it. The little pain is gone." Starber barked and licked Tibby's nose. The doorbell rang, Starber was barking, and Tibby ran to the front door.

Fogel entered, asking, "Gosh, Tib, what's going on?"

Tibby grabbed Fogel, whispering, "I'll tell you in my bedroom."

Tibby closed his bedroom door, laughing. "Fogel, the

little pain has gone home. She was opening mailboxes and removing the mail while I put Starber on our back porch. That's why the Village Police came to the park. He took us in the police car to the Village Police Department. Mom and my aunt arrived and were angry. I told them what had happened. My aunt blamed me and told my mom she was going home. Hey, Fogel, give me five." There hands met with a smack.

Fogel whispered, "Hey, Tib, I got scared and left the park with Ralphie."

Tibby shook his head, smiling and remembering how Fogel used to bully him. "The police officer helped me get rid of the little pain. I should send him a thank-you card."

Fogel whispered, "Man, Tib, I wish he would help me get rid of Ralphie." They both laughed. "How about the campout?"

Tibby suggested they go to their tree house. Rex was in the backyard, and the boys climbed the tree and crawled through the door. Fogel bragged, "Hey, guys, did you notice I have lost some weight and it's easier to get in here?"

Tibby, grinning, raised his hand, and they locked their fingers together, chanting, "True friends together, always."

Tibby told Rex why Shirley went home. Rex shook his head, whispering, "TB, you got to be kidding me."

Tibby replied, "Okay, guys, I've been thinking about our campout. We need information about Teboy, Elock, and the cave people. Od uoy syug eerga?" (Do you guys agree?) Tibby finished speaking, giggling, while Rex and Fogel nodded their heads, agreeing.

Fogel asked, "You guys still want me to get Darnell to talk?"

Tibby said, "Remember, Fogel, he's a little kid. Okay, here's what we need. We need.groceries for the weekend and to get information about the cave people from Darnell. Fogel can you get food from your dad's store for us? I will attempt to find what we can use to look like the cave people, and later make arrangements with our friend Roscoe. Let's plan to meet here tomorrow and I will bring everything we will need. Od uoy syug eerga?" (Do you guys agree?)

Rex and Fogel nodded their heads, raising their hands. The boys locked their fingers together, chanting, "True friends together, always."

THE CAMPOUT

"Hey, guys, I need your help carrying these feed bags. I got some scissors so we can cut these bags to fit us and some twine to use as belts!" Tibby shouted.

Fogel hollered, arriving on his bike. "Guys, I got my food list for you guys to check."

Tibby snickered. "I also got our hair and tape."

The boys, sitting in the tree house, looked at the feed bags, the food list, and a stack of Halloween costume hair. Tibby grabbed a handful of hair. Removing a roll of clear tape, he fastened the hair on it and put it around his head.

Rex and Fogel rolled on the floor laughing, and Tibby hollered, "Hey, guys, what do you think?"

Rex shouted, "TB, you got to be kidding me!" Fogel nodded his head, giggling and agreeing.

Tibby, looking concerned, asked, "Do you think this can fool them?"

Rex snickered and shouted, "Yeah, right, TB, it scares us!"

Rex and Fogel could see that Tibby was getting angry and stopped giggling.

Tibby looking at both, removed his new head gear, and asked, "Rex, will you try this on and see if it fits you?"

Fogel walked over to Rex, mocking in a girl's voice, "Hey, guy, can I have this dance?"

Rex shouted, "You have to wear one!"

Tibby interrupted. "The hair will work, now we have to cut the feed bags to fit around our bodies like the cave people. Let's start with Fogel, who's the heaviest." Tibby placed the bag against Fogel's body and cut the bag to fit around him. Tibby commanded, "Okay, Fogel, pull the bag up over your arms."

Rex smiled at Tibby while Fogel was getting frustrated attempting to put it on. Jumping around caused the tree house to move and creak. Fogel snickered. "Hey, guys, it fits, and I don't need a belt. So, Tib, what do we do about our blue jeans?"

Tibby smiled, shaking his head. "Guys, we don't wear them—only our shorts."

Rex moving toward the door shouted, "TB, you got to be kidding me!"

Fogel was close and grabbed Rex, raising his hand. The boys interlocked their fingers together, chanting, "True friends together, always."

Tibby and Rex cut the feed bags to fit around their bodies and cut the twine to be used as belts to secure the bags, looking like hides around their waists. All three stood in the bags. Tibby grabbed more hair. Now each had long hair, and Tibby whispered, "Guys, the only thing missing now is to get the nformation we need."

Fogel asked, "Hey, Tib, why not now? I will get it from Darnell."

Rex shook his head, moaning, "No, no, no, please no."

Tibby replied, " Tomorrow night is Coley's barbecue. We still need a tent, fishing poles, and camp and sleeping gear. Rex, you've got the fishing poles; Fogel, get any camping equipment you can find at your store. I'll bring a tent. We need the food that is on your list."

Fogel shouted, "I can get all the food we need and much more."

Tibby replied, "Remember enough food for a weekend."

Rex asked, "What about Starber?"

Tibby answered, "I'll take care of it." Starber, hearing his name, pawed at the tree, barking.

Tibby shrugged his shoulders, looking around at his friends and asking, "Okay, we're all set, but we need information about Teboy and Elock. Fogel, you're going to talk to Darnell."

Fogel nodded, replying, "Yeah, Tib, I'll get him to talk."

Tibby nodded his head, sitting down and whispering, "Coley could tell us everything we need to know, but if I talk to her, I need a great excuse. Remember, Rex, how mad she got when we asked her to teach us the cave people's language?"

Rex replied, "TB, she was really upset until her mom reminded her that we couldn't get back in the cave. She's your girlfriend so you can get her to talk. Isn't that right, Fogel?"

Fogel, sounding like a girl, chirped, "Oh yeah, Tibby, I will tell you anything."

Tibby lowered his head, placing his hands on his face, moaning, "Very funny."

Fogel and Rex slapped hands and laughed. Tibby spoke, "If there was just some way to get the information from her. I'll think about it. Maybe Starber can help me. Okay, guys, we meet at the bridge before going to the barbecue. We need to get there in time to set up our camp. Let's meet here tomorrow at four o'clock. Do you guys agree?"

Fogel and Rex nodded their heads, raised their hands, and locked their fingers together. Tibby joined, and the boys chanted, "True friends together, always."

At 4:00 p.m., the boys were in Rex's backyard, and Rex's dad approached them, asking questions. "Rex, Tibby, and Fogel, where are you boys setting up your camp?"

Rex lowered his head, meekly replying, "By the bridge on the north side of the village. We are going to fish in the creek."

Rex's dad looked at each boy and replied, "I didn't know there were fish there."

Tibby cleared his throat, explaining, "I had delivered a

newspaper to the Morcorts' Farm. Rex, Fogel, and I have seen fish swimming in the creek."

Rex's mom approached, asking, "Do you think these boys are old enough?"

Rex moaned, "Mom, we talked about this last night, and you agreed with Dad." She raised her hands and walked away, entering the house.

Rex's dad raised his voice. "You boys be careful. There are snakes. No swimming in the creek, and don't bring any dead fish home, as they smell. Starber, you take care of these guys." Starber barked and jumped on Mr. Tearman as he walked toward the house.

The boys picked up their gear, placed it on their bikes, and put on backpacks. Fogel whispered, "Boy, Rex, I was afraid your dad was not going to let us go."

Rex nodded, agreeing, as Tibby shouted, "Guys, Starber, let's go!"

Parking their bikes at the creek bridge, they walked along the bank, struggling with the heavy backpacks. Rex shouted, "TB, there's a steep bank, and it's flat on top. We will have to climb up that ledge."

Tibby said, "Guys, drop some of your gear here, and we will make several trips."

Rex and Tibby dropped their backpacks but were

amazed when Fogel picked them up and started climbing. Tibby and Rex looked at each other, smiled, and followed Fogel. Arriving at the top, Fogel was sweating and breathing hard and dropped the backpacks. Tibby asked, "Fogel, you okay?" Fogel nodded his head, when the boys heard a strange noise.

Starber stood still, listening, growling, his neck fur standing up. Tibby whispered and motioned, "It's over there."

They climbed up on the rocks, finding a large hole with light, white smoke. Rex asked, "TB, is that a volcano?"

The boys were startled, hearing and seeing a noisy blast of steam. They watched, and about every two or three minutes it would happen. Tibby dropped to his knees, laughing. Rex and Fogel looked at him puzzled when he hollered, "Guys, I got it! I know how Darnell and Coley did it!"

Fogel was curious, asking, "Tib, Coley and Darnell did what?"

Tibby, still smiling, shouted, "Coley and Darnell got out of the cave riding on this steam."

Rex shouted, "TB, you got to be kidding me! No way!"

Tibby demanded, "Fogel, grab the biggest rock you can lift, and throw it."

Fogel asked, "Where?"

Tibby pointed to the opening and replied, "Soon as we hear the noise and see the steam, throw it."

Fogel picked up several rocks and dropped them, and finally found a huge one about the size of Starber. They heard the noise, watched the steam, and Fogel threw it. The boys were amazed watching the rock float as it was pitched from the opening to the ground. Tibby hollered, "Guys, give me five!" and their hands met with a smack. "Rex and Fogel, that's how they got out of the cave. This was Coley and Darnell's elevator. That's why their clothes were dry when they stood by our bikes."

Rex hollered, "Yeah, TB, that's when we were looking for our fishing poles."

Tibby bragged, "I'll bet you I can float like that rock. Watch me." Hearing the noise, watching the steam, he jumped into the opening, floated while sitting, and was pitched, landing on his feet.

Fogel hollered, "Wow, Tib, it's my turn." Rex shook his head, sitting on a rock, and whispered, "Starber, TB and Fogel are nuts. No way would I do that." Starber first jumped on Rex, waiting for the noise, then jumped with Fogel into the opening, floating, and was pitched to the ground, both landing on their feet.

Starber barked, and Fogel shouted, "Oh man, was that cool, like unreal, right, Starber?" Starber jumped around barking, and Rex looked at them shaking his head. Rex was looking around while Tibby, Starber, and Fogel were taking turns jumping into the steam. Rex hollered, and Starber barked. "TB, there's Roscoe!"

The boys watched the huge wave in the creek, and Tibby screamed a loud, high-pitched noise. The wave turned and stopped. The boys and Starber slowly climbed down toward the creek. Tibby asked, "Roscoe, is that you?"

Starber barked, and the boys heard, "Tibby, Rex, Fogel, and Starber, what are you doing? I sure miss you guys, Coley, and Darnell. Do you know where they are, and what they're doing now?"

Fogel, loosing his balance and about to fall in the water below, grabbed a vine, shouting, "Tib, Rex, help me!" Tibby and Rex grabbed him as the vine broke.

Roscoe said, "Fogel, if you fall in the water, I will rescue you." Fogel, standing, patted Tibby and Rex on their shoulders, thanking them. He raised his hand, and the boys locked their fingers together, chanting, "True friends together, always."

Roscoe made his loud, shrill noise. "That's nice that you are true friends. Can I be one of your friends?" Starber jumped on Roscoe, and the boys walked on Roscoe, approaching his wing, locked their fingers together as Roscoe raised his wing, touching their hands, and chanted, "True friends together, always." Starber and the boys returned to the rocks. Tibby asked, "Roscoe, are the cave people still trying to catch you?"

Roscoe replied, "They keep trying with nets, but I get away. I need you and Fogel to keep sinking them."

Tibby replied, "Rex, Fogel, Starber, and I are camping here beside the creek over the weekend. Could you take us back in the cave over the waterfall?"

Roscoe rolled, swam away, and returned, asking, "Why, Tibby, that's a dangerous place. The cave people are bad, and I don't want you, Starber, or your friends to get hurt."

Tibby stood by a rock, explaining about his dream and a great friend, Elock. Darnell, Coley's brother, played with two toys Elock and his machine that looked like a brown bean. Darnell and his friend, a caveman named Teboy, had the toys from the cave that Darnell played with on his porch .

Roscoe laughed, churning the water with his wings and screeching. Rex was curious, asking, "Roscoe, how can you talk to us?"

Roscoe let out another shrill noise and replied, "Darnell

and Coley taught me. I always just made that noise before meeting them in the cave and taking them for rides. Tibby, you remember the day you rescued Darnell from the creek? He was riding me."

Tibby asked, "Roscoe, are there more fish like you in the cave?"

Roscoe slapped his wings, angry, and replied, "The cave people took me from my family at their Tura Land. They placed me in their cave lake here to grow, and then they were planning to eat me. They soon discovered I grew wings, and now they can't catch me. I can't get back to Tura Land with my family." Tibby remembered that Coley had talked about Tura Land being guarded by cave people.

Tibby asked, "Roscoe, did you ever hear the word *Winggots* when you were living there?"

Roscoe swam away and returned, replying, "No, Tibby, when do you want me to take you to the cave lake?"

Tibby replied, "Can you stay in the creek? I will call you."

Roscoe make the loud, horrible noise, replying, "Okay, call me when you're ready. Have you seen Coley or Darnell?"

Tibby replied, "We will be with them later, and I will tell them to meet you at the bridge."

Roscoe hollered, "Okay, all right!"

The boys watched Roscoe swim upstream. Fogel shook his head, giggling, and quipped, "Hey, guys, can you imagine telling someone we just talked to a fish with wings?" The boys laughed, and Starber barked.

THE BARBECUE

The boys and Starber walked from the bridge and up the grassy lane toward Morcorts' Farm. Coley, Darnell, and little TJ ran to greet the boys, and little TJ jumped on Starber.

Coley grabbed Tibby's hand. "I hope you guys are hungry, because Mom has fixed tons of food."

Fogel slapped his hands, replying, "Let me at it. Man, I'm starved."

Rex blurted out, "Darnell and Coley, we just talked to Roscoe, and he told us how much he misses you guys."

Tibby punched Rex, who realized his big mouth might have caused a problem. Coley shouted, "Tibby, why did you hit Rex?" Tibby dropped his head, and both boys snickered.

Coley shook her head, moaning, "I'll never understand boys."

Darnell asked, "Where's Roscoe?"

Fogel replied, "He's in the creek."

Darnell turned away, running toward the bridge.

Arriving at the house, they were greeted by Coley's dad, who was tall , had short hair, muscular build, with a mustache, and wearing coveralls was attending the grill. A small fire was burning by the garden, and Coley's mom motioned for them to join her. She was preparing s'mores. Darnell returned from the bridge all wet, grabbed one from his mom, chomped on it, and shouted, "Oh man, my favorite goodie."

His mom hollered, "Darnell, only one now! There is other food!"

Coley left them, entering the house. Fogel laughed, whispering, "Hey, Tib, that's how I'll get the little runt to talk." Tibby smiled, shaking his head, and Starber was eating a cracker Tibby had given him. Fogel motioned for Darnell to follow him, displaying several of the delicious treats. They walked around the side of the house away from Darnell's parents and sat on some steps.

Darnell whispered, "Hey, Fogel, can I have one of those?"

Fogel crunched on one, smiling, and replied, "Your mom told you only one until you eat other food."

Darnell whispered, "Mom ain't here. Give me that one."

Fogel smiled, holding the morsel close to Darnell, and replied, "Okay, only if you tell me about the cave people and your friend Teboy."

Fogel was in shock when Darnell whispered, "I was with Roscoe a while ago and he told me he's taking you guys back in the cave. If you don't give me that goodie, I'm going to tell Dad, Mom, and Coley."

Darnell smiled while Fogel handed him one. Darnell ate it, demanding, "I know what you guys are doing, and I'm going to tell on you unless you take me with you. I want to see Teboy."

Fogel shook his head, disgusted, and whispered, "You little runt. You stay right here while I call Tib and Rex." Darnell was gloating, jumping around, smiling, and Fogel was getting madder by the second. Fogel motioned for Tibby and Rex while Starber was chasing TJ around the tree. Both jumped on Darnell. Fogel, mad, explained. "Tib, Rex, the little runt is going to cause us a real problem."

Tibby stood on the steps, looking at Darnell, who

smiled, whispering, "Roscoe told me you're going back in the cave, and I'm going with you guys or I'll tell Dad, Mom, and Coley."

Tibby glared at him, and Rex lowered his head, moaning, "Oh no, no, please no."

Darnell saw another goodie in Rex's hand and demanded it. Rex shook his head and started to eat it when Darnell jumped up, hollering, "Dad, Mom, Coley!"

Fogel whispered, "Rex, give the runt the goodie."

Darnell's dad and Coley approached the boys. Darnell walked away to the side of the house, eating the morsel. Darnell returned, jumping up and down with excitement, shouting, "Tibby, Fogel, and Rex want me to stay with them at their camp. Can I, Dad, please?"

Mr. Morcort looked at the boys, asking, "Is that right? You boys want Darnell to stay with you?" Starber barked and TJ whined. Coley walked over to Tibby and kissed him, thanking him.

Darnell's dad continued. "Where's the camp?" Tibby explained they were on the backside of the farmhouse by the creek, on a slope where they could fish in the water.

Darnell moaned, "Please, Dad, please, Dad."

Mr. Morcort smiled, replying, "I think it's great you guys want to take Darnell with you. I guess that will be okay. Darnell, you go tell Mom where you're going tonight, and there will be no swimming in the creek or riding Roscoe." Darnell jumped up and down and ran toward the garden. Coley's dad went back to the grill. The boys thanked Coley's dad and mom for the food. Fogel told them, "I sure enjoyed those big steaks." Tibby and Rex agreed.

Darnell walked from the house with his backpack. Starber jumped on Darnell, and Coley grabbed little TJ. The boys walked toward the bridge, and Fogel grabbed Darnell, holding him tight. Darnell moaned, "Ouch, that hurts. What are you doing?"

Fogel whispered, "You little runt, you're with us now, and you better listen."

Tibby whispered, "Easy, Fogel. Let's allow him to be our friend." The boys lifted Darnell, holding his hand, and locked their fingers together, chanting, "True friends together, always."

Darnell asked, "Am I your friend now?" Tibby, Rex, and Fogel laughed, and Starber barked. The boys arrived at the camp, and Darnell heard a familiar noise, shouting, "It's the Great Fountain!"

Tibby motioned for Darnell to climb with him. They peeked over the ridge into the huge opening, and Tibby asked, "Darnell, is that how you and Coley got out of the cave?"

Fogel tapped Rex when he heard the noise, and seeing the steam, he jumped into the opening, floated, and was pitched to the ground.

Darnell hollered, "It's my turn!"

Fogel hollered, "Come on, Rex, it's fun!"

Rex shook his head, snickering, and jumped with Darnell.

Tibby repeated his question. "Darnell, is that how you and Coley would leave the cave?"

Darnell sat on the ledge, explaining, "The cave people call it the Great Fountain. Coley and I would float to the top. Teboy would do it with me."

Darnell jumped off the ledge, shouting, "I and Teboy did it."

It was getting dark. The boys used bug spray and continued to question Darnell when he wasn't jumping into the opening and riding on the steam. Tibby hollered, "Hey, guys, it's getting late, so let's go make a fire, sit, and talk." All agreed, except Darnell, who wanted to stay there and ride on the steam. The boys grabbed Darnell, holding his mouth to quiet him, and carried him down to their camp. Darnell walked around the fire, and Tibby grabbed Darnell, placing him on a stump by the fire. Tibby asked, "Darnell, why did Teboy hide the toys?"

Darnell, shaking, replied, "They belonged to the king's little boy. Teboy was afraid the cave people would find me with them."

Rex blurted out, "You mean there really is an Elock and a machine that's a brown bean?"

Darnell nodded, and Tibby asked, "Elock is in the cave?"

"Somewhere, I guess."

A light wind was causing the small fire to spread its flames and throw hot ashes into the air. Tibby was concerned. "Hey, guys, we better put this fire out before it spreads with this wind. Darnell, what time do most of the cave people sleep?"

Darnell looked at Tibby, Rex, and Fogel, replying, "I don't know."

Tibby smiled, thinking, *Oh yeah, he's only six.* "You guys ready to go exploring?"

Rex hollered, "TB, you got to be kidding me."

Fogel walked over to Rex. "Look, we all planned this adventure, and I carried your gear up here. We are all going in the cave. I ain't scared of the cave people."

Darnell shouted, "Rex, they can't hurt you if they don't see you."

55

Tibby, scratching his head, asked, "Darnell, what did you say?"

The boys were amazed listening to Darnell talk about a cavewoman called Doctor Zing. He told them, "The doctor was named Zing by the cave people because she used a magic stick. I got sick one time, and the king had the doctor see me. She put the stick over me, there was a zing noise, the tip was like a bright light, and I wasn't sick anymore."

Fogel spoke. "Why didn't you steal the stick, you little runt?" Tibby, Rex, and Fogel laughed, and Starber barked and jumped on Darnell. "Hey, guys, look what the little runt brought in his backpack!" Fogel held up two small toys.

Rex moaned, "Oh no, not Elock and the brown bean machine."

Tibby asked, "Darnell, why did you bring those?" Rex and Fogel laughed, Starber barked, and Darnell started screaming, believing Fogel was going to pitch the toys in the creek.

Darnell begged, "Please, Fogel, don't do it. I have to give them back to Teboy."

Tibby hollered, "He's right, Fogel! Those toys really, really, might help us find Elock!" Tibby hung his head, disgusted, whispering, "I hated hearing Shirley say *really, really, really*, and I just said it." Starber barked and jumped on him.

VISITORS AT THE CAMPOUT

The boys heard someone walking toward the camp, and Starber growled, barked, and ran toward something. They were amazed when they saw Starber jumping on Coley, who announced, "Don't get mad because a girl is at your camp! I was told by Dad and Mom to check on Darnell. Darnell, are you okay, or do you need to come home?"

Fogel nudged Darnell, whispering, "You little runt, you need to go home now."

Rex asked, "Coley, have you ever heard of the Great Fountain?"

Coley hollered, "Darnell, what did you tell them?"

Darnell moaned, "You know about the Great Fountain. It pushed us out of the cave."

Coley, now angry, demanded, "Tibby, why are you asking my little brother these questions?"

Darnell hollered, "They are going in the cave!"

Tibby smiled. "Coley, you remember telling me about your brother's imagination?"

Darnell hollered, "It's true; ask Roscoe!"

Coley entered the tent, noticing the weird gear on the floor. She found the feed bags, black Halloween hair, and tape. Coley grabbed some of the items and approached Tibby, asking, "Is this why you came here? For me to teach you the cave people's language? Darnell, you come home with me now. Tibby, Fogel, Rex, and Starber, I am begging you, please don't go back in the cave. The cave people don't understand us and might hurt you. They wouldn't let our family leave because they are afraid of the outside world. You will be captured and won't be able to leave. So please don't go back in the cave. Please promise me, Tibby."

Coley stopped talking when they heard and observed a helicopter circling above them. The craft landed above the ridge. Starber growled and barked as the large propeller stopped, doors opened, and two men jumped from the craft. The men were shining a bright light around, focusing it on the kids, the tent, and Starber. One man shouted, "You kids stay there! We won't hurt you!"

The man shining his light worked his way down the rock ledges while shouting, "Will your dog bite?"

Coley grabbed Darnell, demanding, "Darnell, you come home with me now!"

The strange-looking man approached the boys' camp. "Hi, I am Professor Dan Quizzley from Genoris University. The other man with me is Mac, our pilot."

Tibby grabbed Starber, who continued growling.

Rex whispered, "TB, should we run?"

Fogel walked up to the man, facing him and announcing, "This is our camp. What do you want?"

The man introduced himself again. "I am Professor Dan Quizzley." The man was old, wearing a baseball cap and glasses, had a beard and mustache, wore a long dark coat, and carried a black backpack. He placed his hands close to the smoking embers, and then pointed above the campsite. "It's dangerous above those rocks. There is steam seeping from the earth."

Darnell shouted, "That's the Great Fountain!"

Professor Quizzley looked at Darnell, asking, "Son, what did you say?"

"That's my brother, with a huge imagination," Coley reported.

The boys laughed, and Starber barked. Starber was growling not at the professor but someone walking toward their camp. "What is going on, Coley? Mom and I heard and watched that helicopter land, and we were getting concerned about you, Darnell, and the boys."

The professor approached Mr. Morcort, with his arm extended. They shook hands, and the professor said, "I am Professor Dan Quizzley from Genoris University, and the other man with the helicopter is Mac, our pilot. We are sorry we disturbed your family, but we are concerned about the steam seeping from the earth, which could indicate an erupting volcano. The state governor has requested an investigation. I believe this is a dangerous place and that your kids and their camp are in danger. Um, Mr. Morcort, do you live in the farmhouse on that hill above the bridge? You are also in danger."

Mr. Morcort shook his head, smiling, and replied, holding Darnell and Coley's hands. "Yes, we live in the farmhouse. Our family has lived here many years. We have seen the steam seeping from the earth, and it was never dangerous before. Why is it dangerous now?"

The professor shook his head, pointing toward some level rocks. "Mr. Morcort, please come with me. I want you to see this."

Tibby, Rex, Fogel, and Starber followed them, while Darnell and Coley sat beside the smoking embers igniting into a small fire. The professor pulled a small steel pole with a metal box attached from his backpack and placed it on the flat surface. Placing the pole in a rock crevice, he opened the box, which contained a meter and a small dial. He explained, "This is why I am concerned. You can see this instrument is showing us how the earth is presently vibrating, and a volcano could erupt here. Steam is seeping from the earth, and this is about to become an active volcano. I'm concerned about these kids, their camp, and your family in the farmhouse. I plan to bring back with me our smartest university students to study this problem. You kids need to leave here now, and I would suggest that your family move to another location until we complete our study. We may have to evacuate the village. I am going to use this meter and several more to see if they also show a disturbance."

Mr. Morcort, Tibby, Rex, Fogel, and Starber walked

back to the smoldering fire. They watched the professor climb up and place more meters at different locations. He removed each meter, hollering, "All the meters are indicating serious vibrations right here in the earth now!"

Returning to the helicopter, he hollered, "Mr. Morcort, please move your family to safety!" They watched the helicopter circle the creek and disappear.

Mr. Morcort shook his head, asking, "I wonder if the professor knows about the cave people?" Looking at Tibby, Fogel, and Rex, he demanded, "You boys have not told anyone about our big secret, have you?" The boys shook their heads, and Starber barked. Mr. Morcort whispered, "The professor will be back with more people. I guess we are going to have to return to the cave and warn King Daggerdash about a volcano eruption. Coley, call Roscoe. Let's talk to him."

The helicopter headed south, and Mac asked, "Professor Quizzley, do you believe there will be a volcano eruption?"

Lowering his head and putting his hands on his face to hide a smile, he replied, "Mac, I don't like what my meters are showing. A volcano eruption could destroy this entire area, including the village. We have to get back here tomorrow. I, with some of our smartest students, can recheck these meters to study this area to determine if a volcano eruption is coming."

Coley was making that horrible, screeching, weird noise, calling Roscoe, and Fogel hollered, "There's the wave!" The huge wave stopped below Coley, who was sitting on an overhanging rock. She carefully leaned forward with a greeting. "Roscoe, it's been way too long. I have missed you. How are you doing?"

The screeching noise caused everyone to plug their ears, and Starber looked down, barking.

Roscoe stopped the noise, splashed the water with his wings, and replied, "Coley, how are you? Darnell, Tibby, Rex, Fogel, and Starber are returning to the cave. Are you going too?"

Mr. Morcort approached Coley while looking down in the water. Coley assured her dad that Roscoe was below her.

Mr. Morcort said, "Roscoe, thank you again for helping us escape out of the cave. Have you returned to the cave lake, and are you aware of any weird vibrations?"

Roscoe made another loud screeching noise and replied,

"I've been living in this creek, but there's not much food here. I stayed away from the cave after your escape. The cave people are always trying to catch me with their nets."

Mr. Morcort walked over to the boys and Starber. Tibby asked, "Mr. Morcort, you heard Professor Quizzley tell us about a possible volcano eruption, so what are we going to do? The cave people could be hurt or killed. Roscoe and Coley have told us about the dangers returning to the cave. We brought to our camp several items to try to fool the cave people."

Mr. Morcort looked at Coley and the boys and walked toward the tent. "Let's see what you boys brought. Coley, tell Roscoe to be careful but sneak back in the cave lake. We may need his help once again to escape. Fogel, we will have to remove the boards covering the barn floor door. The cave people would be safe in their Tura Land far away from here."

Tibby, Rex, and Fogel were talking to each other, and Starber was barking and jumping on Tibby. Rex hollered, "TB, Starber is trying to tell us to go home right now!"

Tibby agreed, replying, "We have to tell our parents and warn all the village people."

Fogel shouted, "Our homes and families are in danger, and we have to tell them now!"

Mr. Morcort announced, "The professor said he was contacting the governor. He will notify the Village Police, who will move the people to safety. We should return to the cave and talk with King Daggerdash. I've taught him English, and we must see him. Maybe we can convince him to move his people to Tura Land. I believe if we go with them, we would all be safe. I have to talk to the king." Mr. Morcort's tone changed. "Coley, Darnell, you boys, come with me to the house—now!"

There was a splash and a screeching, then they heard Roscoe speak. "Coley, I will return to the cave lake, and if you need my help, make this noise." The noise continued in the darkness. Tibby picked up Darnell's backpack with the toys, and they all walked toward the farmhouse.

Rex whimpered, "Please, TB, let's go home now." They passed the farmhouse as Mrs. Morcort approached them. Mr. Morcort told his wife what had happened. They had to warn King Daggerdash and the cave people. They would be safe if they went with the cave people to Tura Land. Everyone was standing in the barn stall. Starber was playing with little TJ. Coley's dad and the boys removed the boards securing the barn floor door.

Rex was trembling. "TB, Fogel, Mr. Morcort, I really

don't want to go down there." Standing over the open door, Rex was moaning and repeating, "I really, really want to go home now."

Tibby shook his head and whispered, "Gosh, Rex, you sound like my little cousin Shirley."

Coley raised her hand and motioned for her parents' hands so they could join her. She chanted, "True friends together, always." Starber pawed at TJ. Coley's dad and mom moved down the steps with flashlights, and soon everyone was soon back in the cave. They could see and hear the cave waterfall, and climbing over several rock ledges, they saw the beautiful colors from the water spray. They heard noises and watched Roscoe fly down the waterfall. TJ was barking, and Starber was growling when they saw several cave men with a fishing net running toward the tunnel.

Fogel giggled, shaking his head, asking, "Hey, Tib, do you think the cave people will ever give up trying to catch Roscoe?"

Rex moaned, "They probably saw us. We're in trouble, and I want to go home now."

"We need no-sees-em from cave rats." moaned Darnell.

Coley's dad, holding Mrs. Morcort's hand, whispered, "Stay close; we are going in the tunnel and down the steps."

The helicopter with professor Dan Quizzley and the pilot arrived at the university. The professor went to his office and called his brother. "Hey, little brother, we have a problem. There's some farmer's nosy kids camping, and the farmer is living in the old Morcort place by the creek. I think I got rid of them. I used some gravity meters telling them there could be a volcano eruption. They bought my story. Ha-ha! We have to move fast to find those rocks. Tomorrow, I'm going back there with my smartest students. You told me old man Morcort gave you one rock for you to pay the paperboy by mail, with a nice tip each week, to deliver the newspaper to his house. Remember when I was in your office, you were laughing and showed me that rock from your safe? Boy, that was a beauty. Yeah, little brother, you were bragging that it could pay for all the newspapers in the country with a huge tip for several thousand years. You're sure, little brother, that the rocks are out there? You better be right, little brother, and we better find those rocks. We are exploring at the university's expense. Do you hear me, little brother?"

The professor got no reply and believed his brother

hung up the phone. There was a pause, and Professor Quizzley slammed his phone down on the desk, laughing.

Mr. Morcort stopped everyone on the steps, giving an order. "I will do all the talking to the cave people; is that understood?"

Coley whispered, "Dad, what if we see our friends. Can't we talk to them?"

Nodding, he demanded, "Okay, but you don't talk to anyone you don't know. Let's stay together."

The rock steps in the tunnel curved, and Rex whispered, "TB, Fogel, that's the noise from when we were riding the steam wave."

Tibby whispered, "Coley, did you and Darnell ride on it?"

Coley smiled, holding TJ and Tibby's hand, when Darnell whispered, "It's a fast way out of the cave. It's fun. Teboy was scared, but I liked riding it."

THE GREAT FOUNTAIN

Slowly they moved down the curving rocks. The boys were amazed at the depth and height of the cave. They stopped walking and looked at the Great Fountain, and Mr. Morcort whispered, "We can't stop here; we have to find King Dag- gerdash."

Fogel grabbed Tibby, pointing at the brilliant rocks along the fountain, whispering, "Tib, check out those spar- kling rocks around the fountain."

Coley heard Fogel and explained, "There are many rocks down here, and the cave people call them dlog (gold). Tibby, the cave people made our family live here so we wouldn't tell anyone. When we get farther down in the cave, you might see more. The king and his son wear the rocks on their wrists and around their necks. The cave people are forbidden to remove any rocks or wear them."

Rex hollered, "Come on, Tibby, Fogel, Starber! Let's get out of here!" Rex ran, climbed up the sparkling rocks on the fountain, heard the steam noise, and leaped into the steam, which carried him to the top cave opening, where he disappeared.

Coley held Tibby's hand tight, pleading, "Tibby, please don't you, Fogel, and Starber leave us. Please stay with me and my family."

Coley's dad approached, asking, "What's going on? We just saw Rex blown out of the cave! We are here, and we can't help him if he is hurt. What are we going to do?"

Coley answered, "Dad, Rex is okay. Darnell and I used the steam cloud to exit the cave numerous times."

Fogel responded, "Mr. Morcort, we were riding it earlier before you arrived at our camp. Rex will be okay, and he will be able to tell his parents and the village people about the volcano erupting."

"Dad! Mom!" Rex hollered, dropping his bike in the backyard and running to the door.

Turning on the porch light and opening the door, Mr. and Mrs. Tearman looked at their son, who was sweating, wheezing, quivering, and stammering, "A volcano!" He fell to the ground.

Marge Tearman looked at her husband, who was carrying Rex, and shouted, "I told you they were to young to camp!"

Rex, getting his breath while in his dad's arms, mumbled, "The volcano, we have to warn the village."

He sat Rex on the sofa, asking, "Son, what are you saying? Marge, get our boy a glass of water!"

Rex gulped water from the glass, and it ran down his neck, mixing with the sweat. Rex hollered, "Dad, over by our camp is a volcano about to erupt. We have to tell everyone."

Rex's dad looked at him, demanding, "Where are your friends, Rex?"

Rex jumped off the sofa, trembling, in tears, and shouting, "Dad, Mom, please, we have to tell everyone in the village to leave! A volcano by our camp is going to erupt and everyone will die."

"Rex, where are Tibby, Fogel, and Starber? Why aren't

they here with you? What's going on? I want to know now!" demanded Mr. Tearman.

Marge spoke softly. "Rex, listen to Dad. We want to help you and your friends. Honey, please tell Dad where your friends are and why they are not with you."

Taking another big sip of water, trembling, shaking, and in tears, Rex replied, "Tibby, Fogel, and Starber are with the Morcorts. I left them to warn you and the village people about the volcano."

Shaking his head and looking at his wife, Mr. Tearman spoke. "Rex, it's okay. Tell us about the volcano."

Rex stood up, handing the glass to his mom and wiping the sweat from his forehead, and he pleaded, "Dad, Mom, we have to alert the village and leave here. A volcano by the creek and next to Morcorts' farm is about to erupt, and we will all be killed."

Mr. Tearman continued. "Rex, what volcano? There is none around here."

"Yeah, Dad, you told me there were no big fish in the creek, and guess what? We not only saw them but tried to catch one. Dad, Mom, earlier tonight a college professor—a Mr. Quizzley from Genoris University—arrived at our camp by helicopter. He put some kind of meters in the rocks and told us the vibrations indicate a volcano eruption. Dad, we have to leave here now and warn the village!"

"Oh my God," Marge moaned, dropping down on the sofa. "Have you boys been taking drugs?"

Mr. Tearman grabbed the phone, calling the Village Police Department. He heard, "Village Police Department. Can I help you?"

"This is Wade Tearman. Is Chief Boyd there?"

"Mr. Tearman, the chief is still in his office. I'll get him for you. Hold on, please."

"Wade, is that you? You still sacking grain at the village mill? How's it going? It's been a long time since we have talked. What's going on?" asked Chief Boyd.

"Chief Boyd, I know you are busy, but we have a problem. Some boys may be missing, and I wonder if you could stop by our house?" reported Wade Tearman.

"Wade, I was just about to leave here when you called. I'm on my way home, so I'll stop by. Did you say some boys are missing? See you in about ten minutes," replied Chief Boyd.

Rex's dad said, "Rex, Village Police Chief Boyd will be here in a few minutes, and you can tell him what you have told us."

Rex shook his head and finished drinking the glass of

water. Lying down on the couch, Rex continued crying and whimpered, "Dad, you and Mom don't believe me, do you?"

Marge replied, "Honey, Dad and I believe something has happened to you and the boys. Dad called Chief Boyd so you can talk to him."

Mr. Tearman said, "Son, Mom is right. We believe you, and we want you to talk to my friend Chief Boyd. He will know what to do. Why don't you wash up?"

The door bell rang, and Mr. Tearman announced, "Rex, Marge, this is Chief Boyd."

Rex sat on the sofa, looking at the man in a blue suit, a gold badge, blue shirt, and a tie held in place by small gold handcuffs. The man was muscular and taller than Mr. Tearman.

Chief Boyd sat down and started talking. "Rex, your dad tells me you're concerned about a volcano eruption. Is that right, Son?"

Rex looked at the floor, moving his legs several times and looking at his dad and mom. "A college professor, Quizzley, told us that a volcano was about to erupt and we should leave our camp. He was in a helicopter that landed above us. He placed some kind of meters in the rocks and told us to leave at once."

Chief Boyd asked, "Who is this Quizzley?"

Rex replied, "He told us he was from Genoris University. He left in the helicopter."

The chief looked at Rex's dad, smiling, and asked, "Where are the other boys you were with?"

Rex shook his head several times and grabbed his legs. "They are with the Morcorts. Tibby has a girlfriend, Coley Morcort. I left them to come home and warn everyone about the volcano eruption."

The chief shook his head several times and announced, "The only Quizzley I know is the manager of the Village Bank. I wonder if he is related to the professor?"

Mr. Tearman stood up, replying, "Yes, we know the bank manager. Chief Boyd, do you think they are related?"

The chief looked at Rex. "Are the boys still at the Morcorts?"

Rex nodded, repeating, "That's where I left them."

The chief demanded, "Son, why weren't those boys concerned enough to come with you and warn their families?"

Rex moaned, "They can't and may never be able to go home."

Mr. Tearman, who had been quiet and listening, shouted, "Rex, what are you saying?"

Before he could continue, Chief Boyd interrupted. "Son, why won't the boys be able to come home?"

Rex cried, his mother was attempting to hold back tears, and his dad whispered, "Do we need to get an attorney?"

Rex blurted out, "Dad, the Morcorts, Tibby, Fogel, and Starber are in a cave probably captured by cave people!"

Chief Boyd smiled shook his head.

Mr. Tearman was approaching Rex, motioning with his finger, demanding, "Rex, you're talking to the Village Police chief about cave people?"

Marge Tearman continued to shake her head, and tears were flowing as she whispered, "Oh my, I can't believe this is happening."

Rex sobbing, pleading, looked at his mom, dad, and Chief Boyd. "Why won't you believe me? People are living in a cave under the Morcorts' barn. A stairway in their barn leads to a cave. The Morcorts, Tibby, Fogel, and Starber are with them to warn the cave people's King Daggerdash about the volcano erupting and to move their people to safety." Rex took another sip of water from a second glass. "The cave people had captured the Morcort family and wouldn't let them leave for years. Tibby, Fogel, and Starber rescued them with Roscoe's help. Roscoe is a big talking fish."

Chief Boyd interrupted. "Son, there was no one living on the farm after old man Morcort died. A Morcort family recently moved into the old place. Son, you are telling us that this family was captured and held by cave people?" Chief Boyd scratched his head. "Why aren't you with your friends in the cave?"

Rex looked at his mom, who was leaning forward in the chair, about to fall, and he jumped up from the couch and grabbed her, asking, "Mom, are you okay?" His mom leaned back in the chair, and Rex continued talking. "We came across the Great Fountain, which provides a steam shaft leaving the cave. I jumped in it and rode it to the surface." Rex looked at his dad, mom, and Chief Boyd and hollered, "I know you don't believe me, so I will show you!"

Chief Boyd smiled and replied, "Okay, Son, you take us there right now."

THE WARNING

Tibby grabbed Darnell. He held him and whispered, "Darnell, earlier you asked us what if the cave people can't see you. What were you trying to tell us?"

Coley asked, "Darnell, what did you tell Tibby? My brother has a great imagination." Darnell jumped around, attempting to get away, but Tibby held on. Fogel grabbed Darnell, who continued kicking and struggling.

Mr. Morcort approached the boys, asking, "Darnell, why are you acting like that?"

Tibby replied, "Darnell knows how to keep the cave people from seeing us."

Mr. Morcort, now curious, continued. "Darnell, you told us about riding on a Roscoe, and we didn't believe you until Coley confirmed it. We believe you know how to keep the cave people from seeing us. Tell us what we have to do."

Darnell begin muttering, "No-sees-um. We have to find no-sees-um. Tibby, Fogel, let go of me so I can find it." Darnell jumped up and climbed up on some rocks and began digging into the crevices with his hand. He placed his hand in one, and everyone was amazed watching Darnell remove a glob of dark greenish goop—and there was no hand.

Coley, terrified and almost in tears, grabbed Darnell, saying, "That stuff is eating your hand."

Darnell laughed and grabbed her with his invisible hand, proving all was okay. Darnell whispered, bragging, "This is how I and Teboy got out of the cave and the cave people couldn't see us. You put it on, and the cave people can't see you. You put it all over you. It would wash off when I rode Roscoe in the cave lake. The goop is in some of the holes between the rocks. I found it when I was trying to catch a no-sees-um."

Tibby interrupted, "What is a no-sees-um?"

Coley whispered, "If you see one, it looks like a rat and when it goes into it's nest it's invisible. The cave people believe if you see one and catch it, you will become a great hunter and have a wonderful life."

Fogel asked, "You mean like good luck?"

Coley nodded, and Darnell bragged, "I saw one, and almost caught it, but it ran into a hole. I reached in and pulled out some goop. I couldn't see my hand, but my hand was there. I put the goop all over me and my friend Teboy. We walked by the king's guards and into the king's room. We scared the king's boy, Little Dash, grabbing the toys he called Elock, and Elock's machine resembling a brown bean."

Tibby nodded and asked, "Are those the toys you hid in the barn floor?"

Darnell replied, "Yep."

Mr. Morcort waved his hands, whispering, "Be careful, but check the rock crevices to find this goop."

TJ didn't like it on him, and he tried to lick it off. Starber didn't care, and soon all were invisible. Mr. Morcort gave orders to the group. "Stay away from water. If you need to talk, you must whisper. Please carry the dogs, and keep them quiet."

Tibby whispered, "I've got Starber."

Coley whispered, "I've got little TJ." Slowly they walked

past the Great Fountain on a narrow path between huge rock ledges. Fogel wanted to holler *wow* but didn't dare. Tibby couldn't believe what he was seeing. There was fire with a horrific sulfur smell, leaping high between the rock ledges. Getting closer the boys could see the fire burning on the end of long poles extending from the rock ledges above, lighting a path. Several cave boys were walking from a tunnel on the path, heading toward the Morcorts, Tibby, Fogel, Starber, and little TJ.

Mr. Morcort whispered, "We must move to the side of the path so the boys can pass by us. Keep the dogs quiet."

The cave boys were getting close, talking and laughing, when Darnell dropped down on the path, rolling fast toward the cave boys, knocking them down. The boys stood up hollering and began fighting. Darnell stood up laughing, making a weird noise, and scared the cave boys, who ran into a tunnel, screaming. Mr. Morcort, hearing Darnell, reached around and grabbed him, whispering, "Darnell, why did you do that?"

Darnell jumped up and down, moaning, "They are bullies. Dad, they tormented me and Teboy."

Tibby snickered, raising Fogel's hand, whispering, "That was you, Fogel."

Fogel replied, "Tib, you're right and never again."

Raising his hand with Tibby's hand, Fogel whispered, "True friends together, always."

The cave boys returned from the tunnel with other cave people who were carrying swords and spears. Pointing toward the path, the cave boys hollered, "Ereth, ereth, ereth!" (There, there, there.) Several of the cave people were moving around, waving their spears, and making noise. One big cave man walked from the tunnel, and the cave boys were laughing and daring him to walk up the path. The big man left them, approaching the area where the cave boys had fallen and heard that scary noise. The big man made a weird sound that puzzled the cave boys.

"Darnell, Darnell, Darnell, you here?"

The cave boys were pointing and laughing and returned to the tunnel with the cave people. The big man continued speaking. "Darnell, Darnell, Darnell, Darnell, you here?"

Darnell jumped away from his dad and grabbed Teboy's hand, whispering, "Teboy, s'ti em, Darnell." (Teboy, it's me Darnell.) "M'i htiw ym dad, ym mom, Coley, dna ruo sdneirf." (I'm with my dad, my mom, Coley, and our friends.) "Uoy t'nac ees su." (You can't see us.) "Ew desu on-sees-mu." (We used no-sees-um.) Darnell asked, "Dad, can Teboy come with us if he gets no-sees-um and can't be seen?"

Mr. Morcort whispered, "Teboy could help us. Darnell, help him find the no-sees-um in the rock crevices."

Fogel whispered, "Tib, we can now talk to Teboy."

Coley replied, "Thanks to Darnell." Coley squeezed Tibby's hand. "Teboy is big, but he is Darnell's best friend." They watched as Teboy—with long braided hair and a long beard, wearing a hide covering over his chest and continuing around his waist, and in bare feet—jumped up on the rock ledges.

Teboy and Darnell climbed higher on the rock ledges, looking for no-sees-um. Teboy pulled some goop from the crevices, and with Darnell's help Teboy slowly placed it on his body, becoming invisible. Holding Teboy's hand Darnell approached Tibby and Fogel, whispering, "Tibby, Fogel, this is Teboy with me, who is my friend. I taught Teboy English. Teboy told me he wants to shake your hands." Tibby, Fogel, Darnell, and Teboy held hands.

Tibby, holding Coley's hand, whispered, "True friends together, always."

Mr. Morcort asked, "Is anyone wearing a watch and can tell me the time?"

Tibby looked at his wrist but couldn't see his watch. "Mr. Morcort, I can't see my watch, but the last time I looked at my watch, the time was nine o'clock."

The whispering continued as Mr. Morcort commanded, "We wait here until the cave people are asleep. We will then wake King Daggerdash and tell him about the volcano eruption."

Mr. Tearman, Rex, and Police Chief Boyd arrived at the bridge by Morcorts' farm and saw Tibby and Fogel's bikes. Rex said, "Dad, our camp is over on a slope by the farm. Above our camp is the Great Fountain, with the steam coming from the cave that I rode to leave the cave."

Chief Boyd, smiling and winking at Mr. Tearman, replied, "Okay, Son, show us." They followed Rex with flashlights to the camp. Rex showed them inside the tent the black Halloween hair they would use to fool the cave people. Rex took them to the top of the slope and jumped into the steam, sitting down, and was thrown to the side of the opening. Mr. Tearman grabbed his son and held him, hugging him and saying, "Rex, I am sorry that I didn't believe you. Please, Son, forgive me and your mom."

Chief Boyd agreed, asking, "Son, how do we get into

the cave?" They followed Rex into the Morcorts' barn. They found the barn floor door open and with flashlights proceeded down the stairs. Upon entering the cave, Rex whispered, "Follow me, and whisper when you talk."

Chief Boyd and Mr. Tearman were amazed looking at the colors in the waterfall and seeing the cave lake. Rex made a harsh screeching noise to call Roscoe. Chief Boyd whispered to Mr. Tearman, "Didn't your son tell us to whisper?" Mr. Tearman nodded when they noticed big waves in the lake. Something big was approaching Rex.

Chief Boyd grabbed his revolver, pointing it toward the something, and Rex shouted, "Dad, stop Chief Boyd from shooting his gun! Please, Chief Boyd, don't shoot! It's okay! Roscoe is a friend!"

Mr. Tearman whispered to the chief, "Do you believe this? Are we dreaming, or is this really happening?" Chief Boyd continued to point his gun on the something, and the wave stopped by Rex. Both Mr. Tearman and Chief Boyd were looking at each other, shaking their heads in disbelief, listening to the something in the cave lake talking to Rex.

"Rex, is that you?"

Rex replied, "Yes, Roscoe. Please stay close by, as we may need your help to leave here."

Roscoe slapped his wing in the water. "Rex, you were

with Tibby, Fogel, Coley, Darnell, and Mr. Morcort. What happened? Why aren't you with them now?"

Rex replied, "I left them to warn our village about a volcano eruption." The wave moved, and there was a splash.

Roscoe replied, "I remember about Coley's dad asking me if I knew about vibrations in the water. I wish I was back home in Tura Land. Rex, who is with you shining the bright light in my eyes?"

"Roscoe, this is my dad and the head of our police, Chief Boyd."

Roscoe slapped the water, asking, "Rex, what is a police chief? Is he going to try to catch me, like the cave people?"

Chief Boyd approached Rex, holstering his gun and telling Roscoe, "Roscoe, I promise you, I won't try to catch you."

Roscoe replied, "Rex, I will stay close. Call me if you want me." The wave moved away, making the screeching noise, and disappeared.

Chief Boyd couldn't believe that he had talked to a giant green fish with wings and snickered, shaking his head. "Good grief, I just talked to a fish."

Rex whispered, "Follow me." They followed Rex to a cave tunnel.

Chief Boyd whispered to Mr. Tearman, "I think we should return in the morning, and I will have several police officers with us. I have seen and believe your son is telling us the truth about the cave people." Mr. Tearman agreed and approached Rex, telling him what Chief Boyd had decided.

Rex pleaded, "No, no, no, please, we can't leave here. The cave people may have the Morcort family, Tibby, Fogel, Starber, and Coley's puppy." Mr. Tearman grabbed Rex, hugging him, and followed Chief Boyd to the stairs returning to the barn.

Mr. Morcort announced, "The cave people should be asleep. Let's go!"

Slowly they followed the lighted path. Moving between two huge overhanging rock ledges, they could see small fires protruding from the earth. They walked by the cave people, who were asleep on huge leaf beds close to the fires. Holding on to each other, Mr. Morcort approached a very strange-looking tunnel. Fire from the earth surrounded a platform leading to the tunnel.

Fogel whispered, "Hey, Tib, if you fall here, you're a roasted turkey."

Mr. Morcort whispered, "Be quiet and be careful."

Walking toward the entrance over the platform stood several cave men with spears. While walking past the guards, Darnell punched one in the ribs. The guard fell to his knees, looking at the other guards and trying to determine who hit him. Several guards dropped their spears, attempting to help him stand up. The guards were arguing and hollering at each other. Darnell and Teboy were snickering, and Mr. Morcort heard them. Mr. Morcort whispered, "Darnell, Teboy, please, no more goofing off. Be quiet and follow me."

They walked into a large cave room. There in front of them were two sparkling gold chairs. Fogel whispered, "Tib, check out those chairs. They would look nice in our tree house."

Mr. Morcort whispered, "The chairs belong to King Daggerdash and his son, Little Dash. All of you stand over there, along that cave wall." Mr. Morcort waited a few minutes, then continued. "I will now wake up King Daggerdash." They watched the king lying asleep on a huge leaf close to a fire. The silence was broken with, "Gnik Daggerdash, ekaw pu!" (King Daggerdash, wake up!)

The king sat up, hollering, "Sdraug, sdraug, sdraug! Ohw serad ot ekaw eht gnik?" (Guards, guards, guards!

Who dares to wake the king?) Several guards from the entrance ran to the king, waving their spears and swords. Starber tried to growl, but Tibby kept his hand over Starber's mouth, whispering, "Starber, no, everything is okay."

Coley's little TJ didn't growl but jumped from her arms. Coley, scared, squeezed Tibby's hand, whispering, "Tibby, TJ is loose. He jumped from my arms, and I can't see him."

Tibby raised Starber in his arms to whisper in his ear, "Starber, you have to find little TJ." Tibby placed Starber on the floor and watched the guards, who were jumping around, hollering, grabbing their ankles, and running out of the cave. King Daggerdash hollered, "Sdraug, sdraug, sdraug! Uoy nur morf ruoy gnik?" (Guards, guards, guards! You run from your king?)

The king started to lay down when Mr. Morcort hollered, "Gnik Daggerdash, ruoy sdraug tfel uoy, deracs fo ym rewop." (King Daggerdash your guards left you, scared of my power.) "Gnik Daggerdash, evom ruoy elpoep ot Arut Danl won!" (King Daggerdash, move your people to Tura Land now!)

King Daggerdash stood up and removed his sword, moving it back and forth in the air. He grabbed his ankles, hearing a growling, and jumped back into his bed of leaves. The king hollered for his guards. Several guards entered, moving their spears back and forth in the air. Again hearing growls and grabbing their ankles, they ran from the cave. Tibby, Fogel, Darnell, and Teboy were all trying to keep from laughing while watching the commotion.

King Daggerdash stood up, dropped his sword on the leaves, bowed, and hollered, "Si raeh uoy, Taerg Tirips. Ruoy hsiw si detnarg." (I hear you, Great Spirit. Your wish is granted.)

Coley whispered, "Tibby, where is Starber and my TJ?" Tibby snickered. "They're keeping the guards from entering this cave."

Fogle whispered, "Hey, Tib, check out that king wearing all that gold."

The king was tall, muscular, had dark long hair and bare feet, and his wrists were covered with gold bracelets. A gold necklace hung around his neck. He ran toward the entrance, hollering and grabbing his ankles. Tibby was at the entrance as the king rushed by him, stopping on the platform with his guards.

Tibby whispered, "Starber, Starber, come here now. Good boy, Starber." He picked up Starber, who was jumping on his leg. TJ was jumping on Starber, so Tibby grabbed him by his collar, whispering, "Coley, I have your little TJ."

The king standing on the platform with his guards bowing toward him commanded, "Sdraug, ekaw lla elpoep! Llet elpoep ruoy gnik sdnamed uoy evom ot Arut Dnal won!" (Guards, wake all people! Tell people your king demands you move to Tura Land now!) A small cave boy ran into the king's chambers from a tunnel. The boy resembled the king, with his wrists covered with gold bracelets and a gold necklace hanging around his neck.

Darnell whispered, "Teboy, it's Little Dash, the king's son."

Teboy snickered, replying, "Let's get even with that brat."

Little Dash, hollering and kicking, was lifted high into the air, looking like a kite as he flew toward the king's bed. Little Dash jumped from the king's leaves, screaming, hollering, running, and disappearing in a tunnel. Darnell and Teboy were laughing.

Fogel whispered, "Tib, did you see that? Boy, you and Rex thought I was bad about bullying you, but I never threw you guys in the air."

Mr. Morcort whispered, "Darnell, Teboy, stop teasing Little Dash. The king's guards are waking the cave people. Please, all of you be quiet and don't move around. Coley, Tibby, keep Starber and little TJ quiet. Remember, the cave people can't see us, but they can hear us."

AN ARREST

Fogel's old friend Kurpit Chilling was talking to his friends. "Guys, we have to save Fogel from the goofballs. Fogel's now friends with them. We tried to destroy their tree house with fire. The goofballs stopped the fire but not the mud balls we threw at their tree house. Their fleabag mutt chased us, or we would have decorated them with mud."

Jer, called the Jerk by his friends, was the size of Kurpit but not as tall. "Hey, guys, let's go to the creek and catch some frogs."

Kurpit laughed. "Yeah, man, let's catch some frogs and

put them in the goofballs' tree house. Grab your bikes; let's go."

Kurpit, Jer, and Mac, who was nicknamed Mouse and was short and thin like Kurpit, arrived at the creek bridge dropping their bikes beside Fogel and Tibby's bikes. Kurpit looked at the one bikes telling Jer and Mac, "Hey, guys, this looks like Fogel's bike." The boys raced down to the creek. Running along the creek bank, Kurpit saw a tent. He pointed at it, hollering, "Jerk and Mouse, follow me!" They arrived at the tent, and Kurpit walked into it, hollering, "Hey, guys, check this out," while pointing at a bunch of black Halloween hair, feed bags, and rope. Jer grabbed the black Halloween hair, attempting to put it on Kurpit's head.

Kurpit socked Jer on the shoulder, telling him, "Jerk, knock it off before I knock you to the ground! Hey, Jerk, Mouse, look over here." Kurpit picked up a hat and looked at it. Inside the hat was Fogel's name in black ink. Kurpit put the hat on his head, announcing, "Guys, this is Fogel's hat. That bike on the bridge belonged to Fogel. This must be his or the goofballs' tent, so he's around here somewhere. Let's find him. I'll bet he's with the goofballs." Kurpit had just finished speaking when they heard a loud noise. Racing from the tent, they watched as a helicopter landed in the field above their location. People jumped from the craft and stood in a circle as one older person in the center was talking to them.

The older man hollered, "You boys at the tent, stay there. I need to talk to you." The older man, with several people behind him, climbed down the rock ledges, arriving at the tent. The older man looked at the boys, shaking his head and telling them, "Hi, I am Professor Dan Quizzley." Pointing at the group of people behind him, he continued. "These are our students from Genoris University. You are not the kids with their father I talked to yesterday who were camping here and live in that farmhouse. Who are you? Where are the other kids camping here and their dad?"

Kurpit replied, "We were catching frogs in the creek and spotted this tent."

The professor cleared his throat, talking with authority. "I and my students are here checking for a volcano eruption, and you boys need to leave this area now! Go on; get out of here now!"

Kurpit hollered, "Jerk, Mouse, let's get out of here!"

Jer asked, "What about Fogel and the goofballs?"

Kurpit, snickering, replied, "Okay, Jerk, you go find them. Mouse and I are leaving." Jer quickly change his mind, running with them as the boys raced to the bridge, grabbed their bikes, and rode toward the village.

Professor Quizzley smiled at his students, telling them, "The kids are gone. Now let's find what we came here to find." The students were carrying small pie pans with holes and a straining screen attached. They carefully walked down the rock ledges to the creek. Several minutes passed, and the students determined the creek at their location was to deep to pan for gold. They continued walking along the creek bank, looking for shallow spots.

Village Police Chief Boyd and several other police cars arrived on the bridge. Rex, with his father, was riding with Chief Boyd. Rex hollered, "That's Tibby's and Fogel's bikes!"

Kurpit, Jer, and Mac were riding on their bikes when the police cars passed them, and they spotted Rex in Chief Boyd's car. Kurpit stopped his bike, which also stopped Jer and Mac. "Hey, guys, something big is happening back there at that bridge. I saw one of the goofballs riding in that first cop car that just passed us. Let's go back. Fogel is in trouble." Kurpit, leading Jer and Mac, raced to the bridge. The boys watched as several police officers climbed up the rock ledges toward the helicopter. Several other police officers were entering the old barn by the farmhouse with the goofball and two older men.

At the creek Professor Quizzley was standing on some rocks in the water watching his students drop their pie pans in the water, digging into the dirty muck, pulling it up, and screening it. The professor looked up and saw the police officers walking toward the helicopter and began to panic, realizing the pilot might tell the police about a volcano eruption. The police would be told the students were testing for a volcano eruption, and the police would warn the village residents, county residents, and the governor. The professor, attempting to hide his quivering voice, hollered at his students. "All students go back to the helicopter now! We are wasting our time here! Pitch those pie pans in the creek!" He hollered at the police who were talking to the pilot. "Please wait! I have to talk to you!"

Professor Quizzley climbed the rock ledges with his students. "All of you return to the helicopter while I talk to the police."

Sergeant Jill, with red hair protruding around her police hat, who was small in size, with silver handcuffs and a revolver hanging from her belt, approached the professor, asking, "What did you want to tell us? The pilot told us that you are Professor Dan Quizzley from Genoris University, and these are students here to study and determine if a volcano eruption will happen. I am wondering why your students are carrying pie pans? We could see them dipping the pans in the creek. Looks like they are panning for gold. Isn't that right, Professor Quizzley?"

The professor, attempting to say the correct words and trying not to tremble, blurted out, "There is no volcano eruption. We have determined through our studies, there is no volcano eruption in this area."

Sergeant Jill was not satisfied with the professor's story. She walked to the helicopter, opening the doors and talking to the students. "What were you kids doing with the pie pans down at the creek? Is that how you determine if there is a volcano about to erupt?"

The students laughed, and one boy with curly black hair, tall as the professor, looking big like a center of a football team, stood up. "What volcano eruption? We were in the creek looking for gold as a college project. Here is my pie pan." The students continued laughing. Sergeant Jill shook her head as she closed the craft doors, carrying the pie pan. She walked up to Professor Quizzley, getting close to his face. "Professor, your kids told me they were looking for gold, not a volcano eruption. Here is one of the pie pans that your student didn't pitch in the creek. Our Chief Boyd is with a kid now looking for kids who were camping in a tent. This kid told our chief that a professor from a helicopter told them to leave their campsite because of a volcano eruption. Was that professor you?"

The professor felt like a pin had been pushed into his heart. "It was my brother's idea to scare everyone so we could find gold."

Sergeant Jill opened the cockpit door, instructing the pilot that he could leave but not with the professor. She returned to the professor, telling him, "Chief Boyd alerted the village mayor and the governor about a volcano eruption. This is your lie. Isn't that right, professor?" She then looked at the police officers beside her, ordering, "Take this professor to our village office. Chef Boyd will want to talk with him. Radio the police dispatcher that there is no volcano eruption and to advise the governor and our village mayor."

The police officers grabbed Professor Quizzley, carefully holding his arms while the helicopter lifted into the air. Sergeant Jill and the police walked down the rock ledges toward the creek and arrived at the bridge.

By the bridge Kurpit, Jer, and Mac were watching the police place the professor in the police car's back seat.

Standing by their bikes, Kurpit hollered, "Hey, police, that's the old guy who told us to leave this area when we wanted to catch frogs in the creek. He told us there was going to be a volcano eruption."

Sergeant Jill looked in the police car at Professor Quizzley, shaking her head. "Professor, you've been busy lying about a volcano eruption to find gold, haven't you?" Sergeant Jill told the police officers in the police car, "Arrest this professor right now!"

Kurpit, Jer, and Mac watched the police remove the professor from the car and place handcuffs on his hands, returning him to the car's cage. Kurpit laughed. "Hey, Jerk, Mouse, that will teach the old guy not to lie and scare us. Let's go see what's going on with the goofball in the barn!"

The police car left the bridge with the professor. Sergeant Jill grabbed Kurpit's bike seat, stopping him and standing in front of Jer and Mac. She demanded, "Boys, the barn is police business and now off limits. Go back to the village, or you can still catch frogs in the creek, but stay out of the barn. You are not allowed in the barn, understood? You can catch frogs in the creek but stay out of the barn."

The boys nodded and walked from the bridge down to the creek. Kurpit, Jer, and Mac sat on the creek bank, watching Sergeant Jill standing beside her police car. She was watching them. Kurpit whispered, "That lady cop ain't going to leave, so we can't get into the barn."

Jer replied, "Let's catch some frogs and put them in the goofballs' tree house."

Mac snickered. "Hey, Kurpit, what about their tent?"

Kurpit smiled. "Mouse, we can't do anything with that lady cop standing on the bridge, watching us. Let's take a walk so she can't see us."

The boys walked along the creek passing the tent above on the rock ledge and walked where the creek curved. Kurpit, snickering, said, "Hey, guys, the lady cop can't see us now. Why don't we climb that hill, head into the woods, and circle back to the barn? Maybe we can find a back door where we can get in the barn without that lady cop seeing us." The boys agreed, slapping their hands together, and started walking up the rocky ledges.

King Daggerdash stood on the cave platform, watching the cave people arrive with his guards. The cave people— old, young, and those with many children—circled away from the platform. Many were carrying animal skins that appeared filled with food and water. King Daggerdash, standing in the center of his people, spoke.

"Ruoy gnik saw denekawa by eht Taerq Tirips." (Your king was awakened by the Great Spirit.) He continued. "Taerg Tirips sdnamed ew evom ot Arut Dnal." (Great Spirit demands we move to Tura Land.)

The cave people chanted, "Sey, Taerg Eno." (Yes, Great One.)

King Daggerdash grabbed a guard, telling him, "Og ekaw pu ym nos dna gnirb mih ereh." (Go wake up my son and bring him here.)

The soldier first hesitated at the cave entrance, grabbing his ankles. King Daggerdash shoved him into the entrance. The guard raised his spear, moving it back and forth, and ran past Tibby, who was holding Starber. Fogel and Coley, holding little TJ, were still standing along the wall by the entrance, watching the king and the cave people. The guard ran through the king's chambers, disappearing in the tunnel. After several minutes the guard returned with the king's son, Little Dash, by his side. They ran out the entrance, joining King Daggerdash and the cave people waiting by the platform. Two guards grabbed the king and Little Dash's gold chairs, carrying them.

The Morcorts, with Tibby, Fogel, and Teboy, watched from the entrance as King Daggerdash, his son, and his guards carrying both gold chairs walked away from the platform with all the cave people following them.

The Village Police following Chief Boyd with Rex and his father were surprised entering a cave from the barn steps. The police couldn't believe seeing a waterfall with a display of many colors.

There was the lake and the various rock formations. Rex startled the police, pointing. "We have to go in that tunnel and follow the rock steps."

Chief Boyd replied, "Lead on, Son; we will follow you."

The police, Chief Boyd, and Mr. Tearman couldn't believe what they were seeing. There in front of them was a fountain of steam surrounded by gold rocks. Several officers were whispering, "Check out that fountain."

Rex continued walking by the fountain, leading them toward the opening tunnels where the cave people lived. Rex whispered to the chief, his dad, and the police, "We have to be very quiet so the cave people don't hear us. I left Tibby, Fogel, and the Morcort family at the Great Fountain.

I rode the steam to the opening above the cave. That's how I got out of here."

Chief Boyd stopped the group, whispering, "Men, stay quiet, stay alert, as you may see some cave people." They continued walking the path leading between the rock ledges and the fires on long poles extending from the rock ledges and lighting their path.

The cave people following their king walked downward between the rock ledges, leaving their cave homes.

Mr. Morcort said, "The Great Spirit idea has worked. The king, his son, and all the cave people are on their way to Tura Land, where they will be safe. We won't go with them. We have to leave the cave now and alert the village about this volcano eruption."

The Morcorts, Tibby, Fogel, and Teboy left the king's chambers, walking over the platform with the leaping fires on both sides. Tibby almost fell down, not believing what he was seeing.

Fogel whispered, "Tib, there is Rex with his dad and the Village Police!"

Tibby shook his head, replying, "They can't see us."

Mr. Morcort spoke. "We must stay together, and I will talk to the police."

Rex and his dad were looking in the various tunnels. They could see mats of grass next to fires burning from the earth where the cave people were living. Mr. Morcort approached Chief Boyd, saying, "Village Police, you can't see us, but we are all here with one of the cave people."

Several police officers backed against the rock ledge, raising their guns.

Rex hollered, "Dad, let's get out of here. Quick, run to the Great Fountain. Do what I do, and we will be out of here!" Rex stopped talking and was smiling. He was hearing a familiar sound with Tibby and Fogel laughing. That could only be Tibby and Fogel. Rex, with a quiver in his voice, asked, "Tibby, Fogel, are you here?"

Starber was barking, and little TJ was whining. Rex, excited, hollered, "TB, Fogel, Starber, where are you? Why can't we see you?"

Mr. Morcort answered, "You will see us as soon as we wash in the lake. We are now going to the cave lake. Please come with us. Don't worry about the cave people, as they left with their king some time ago. There is no one here now except us. Please return with us to the cave lake."

Tibby pitched Starber in the water with a splash. The

police, Rex, and his father were amazed at watching a splash turn into Starber swimming toward them. They watched as Tibby, Fogel, Coley, little TJ, Darnell, Mr. Morcort, and Mrs. Morcort became visible. They saw Teboy, looking like a caveman, who was holding hands with Darnell.

The police sat on the rock ledge by the water as Mr. Morcort explained about acting like a great spirit, warning a King Daggerdash about a volcano eruption, and the king moving his cave people to another cave location. Mr. Morcort pointed at Teboy saying. "This boy is our special son."

Teboy, standing in bare feet, continued to hug Darnell. He smiled. "Thank you, Dad, Mom, and Coley." Teboy placed Darnell on his shoulders.

GOING FOR A SWIM WITH SHARKS

Sergeant Jill was surprised seeing Chief Boyd, the police officers, and a group of people all walking from the barn entrance doors, with two dogs following them. Sergeant Jill walked up to the group and stared at Teboy. She started talking to Chief Boyd.

"Chief, we have arrested a Professor Quizzley. The professor admitted to me that he and his brother, who is the Village Bank owner, lied about a volcano eruption. They were scaring everyone away from this bridge and creek to have college students look for gold. I told our police officers to arrest his brother at the Village Bank."

Mr. Morcort, looking tired, walked up to Sergeant Jill, asking, "You are telling us that the volcano eruption is a lie and all about gold?"

Sergeant Jill nodded, asking, "Did the professor tell any of you that there was going to be a volcano eruption?"

Tibby hollered, "Professor Quizzley told all of us that we should leave this area! He told Mr. Morcort that his family should leave the farmhouse!"

Chief Boyd asked, "Sergeant, did you notify the governor and the mayor?"

Sergeant Jill replied, "Our officers took the professor to your office and were told to alert everyone." Sergeant Jill, staring at Teboy, asked, "Who is this?"

Chief Boyd smiled. "This is Teboy, the Morcorts' special son, who was living in the barn."

Sergeant Jill turned her head to look at Teboy several times while walking back to her car.

Chief Boyd announced, "Okay, people, we are done here, so let's return to our village."

Mr. Morcort and Mrs. Morcort thanked everyone, and Mr. Morcort walked over to Chief Boyd, pleading, "Chief

Boyd, will you please tell your police officers not to tell anyone about this cave, the cave people, and the gold? We don't want people coming here looking for a cave with gold and trespassing on our property."

Chief Boyd answered, "We can do that."

Kurpit, Jer, and Mac had walked through the woods above the creek, across the field, and to the backside of the barn. While walking closer to the barn, they noticed a big opening and crawled inside. They had hidden in a stall and watched the police with Tibby, Fogel, Rex, another man, the Morcorts, Starber, little TJ, and Teboy. Their big surprise was seeing Teboy.

Kurpit whispered, "Jerk, Mouse, did you see that guy with Fogel, the goofballs, and the police?"

Jer sneered. "Yeah, man, something big is going on. That big guy looks like a caveman that just came out of the earth."

Mac agreed, shaking his head in disbelief, whispering, "Guys, they came from over there in that stall." Mac pointed at the empty stall. All three boys slowly crawled toward that stall, finding the floor door open with stairs leading down into the dark. Kurpit started down the steps, motioning for Jer and Mac to follow him.

Tibby and Fogel, with Starber at their side, walked to the bridge to get their bikes. However, arriving at the bridge, there were five bikes.

Fogel recognized the bikes, and Fogel hollered at Sergeant Jill, who was backing her car off the bridge. "Eh, Miss Officer, did you see any boys while you were here on the bridge?"

Sergeant Jill pointed toward the creek, saying, "There are three boys your age down by the creek hunting frogs. Do you know the boys?"

"Yes, miss, I believe I do," Fogel replied, describing Kurpit.

Sergeant Jill nodded. "That's one of the boys."

Fogel walked back to Tibby and Starber while the police cars with Rex and his dad were leaving the bridge. Fogel tapped Tibby on the arm. "Hey, Tib, guess what?" Pointing at the one bike, Fogel continued speaking. "That bike belongs to Kurpit, and the other two bikes probably belong to Jerk and Mouse, who are Kurpit's buddies." Starber stood on the side of the bridge on the riverbank, barking. "Tib, the woman cop said that Kurpit, with Jerk and Mouse, are hunting frogs in the creek. Come on, Tib, I owe Kurpit big time for trying to set our tree house on fire." Fogel slapped his right fist into his left hand. Starber was growling. Fogel continued talking. "Tib, we better check our tent. Kurpit, Jerk, and Mouse might have set our tent on fire." Fogel grabbed Tibby, hollering, "Come on, Tib and Starber!"

Tibby, Fogel, and Starber ran down to the creek bank toward their camp. Arriving inside the tent, Tibby reported, "Fogel, no one's been here."

Fogel shook his head again, grabbing Tibby. "Come on, Tib, let's see if we can find Kurpit, Jerk, and Mouse. We owe them big." Again Fogel slapped his right fist into his left hand.

Sniffing along the creek bank, Starber started whining and growling where the creek curved. Fogel approached Starber, spotting in the mud three sets of footprints. Fogel hollered, "Good boy, Starber!" and pointed at the ground. "Hey, Tib, look what Starber has found. There's three footprints belonging to Kurpit, Jerk, and Mouse. They are close, so let's follow 'em."

Slowly they walked, hunting for Kurpit, Jer, and Mac. At a ledge the footprints disappeared. Tibby and Fogel looked at the ground in different places for footprints. Starber started up the ledge, turning around and barking.

Tibby hollered, "Fogel—Kurpit, Jerk, and Mouse climbed that ledge leading into the woods. They saw us and must be hiding in the woods. Starber knows where they are, so let's follow him." Tibby and Fogel followed Starber, climbing up the high rock ledges. They were walking in the brush and woods. Starber surprised Tibby and Fogel when he left them running through a field toward the barn. Starber would stop, turn around, and bark.

Tibby shouted, "Fogel, Starber wants us to follow him!" They ran and were amazed watching Starber disappear through a big hole in the barn. Tibby laughed. "Fogel, that's the hole Rex, Starber, and I made to get out of the barn so Coley and Darnell Morcort wouldn't find us in there. Come on, Fogel, crawl in; it's okay."

Fogel, shaking his head, mumbled, "Tib, I ain't l going in there with spiders."

Tibby, laughing, looked at Fogel and pleaded, "Come on, Fogel," while crawling through the hole. Fogel spit on the barn and followed Tibby. Starber was whining, standing on the steps in the stall below the opening in the floor leading to the cave. Tibby grabbed Fogel, whispering, "Fogel—Kurpit, Jerk, and Mouse have found the cave. Starber is telling us they went down those steps."

Fogel smacked his right fist against his open left hand, replying, "Tib, this is really bad. Kurpit will tell everyone about the cave. I hope he didn't see Teboy. We have to find them. They can't tell anyone about the cave, the cave people, or Teboy. Maybe we should get Coley to go with us back in the cave. Do you agree?"

Tibby replied, "Yes, you're right. Come on; let's get Coley."

Tibby, Fogel, and Starber ran from the barn to the farmhouse and knocked on the door.

Coley appeared surprised to see Tibby, Fogel, and Starber. Coley, smiling, said, "I thought you were going back to the village."

Tibby whispered, "We believe Fogel's ex-friends were in your barn and are now in the cave."

Fogel moaned, "They ain't my friends. Used to be, but no more."

Coley whispered, "Tibby, please don't go back in the cave."

Tibby replied, Coley, you have to go with us. We have to find Kurpit, Jerk, and Mouse."

Coley moved to the steps on the porch and sat down, asking, "Tibby, how do you know those boys were in the barn and took the stairs to the cave?"

Tibby looked at Coley, replying, "We found their bikes on the bridge. Starber tracked them from the creek by our camp to the barn and down the steps leading to the cave."

Fogel, shaking his right fist into his open left hand, stated, "Come on, Tib, let's go find 'em. I owe them a big fist for trying to set fire to our tree house."

Coley gasped, repeating, "Those boys set fire to your tree house?"

Tibby replied, "They also threw mud balls at our tree house and at Starber, hitting him."

Coley, standing, placed her hand in Tibby's hand, attempting to hold back tears. "Tibby and Fogel, I can't go back in the cave with you. Dad and Mom won't allow it. You and Fogel please don't go back in the cave. The cave people might return, finding you. They might hurt you or keep you prisoners like they did to me, Darnell, Dad, and Mom."

Fogel bragged, "I ain't scared of 'em." Starber barked to agree.

Darnell and Teboy opened the door and walked out on the porch. Teboy looked different. His beard was shorter, hair was shorter, and he was wearing a blue shirt. He was in bare feet. A hide was covering his lower body. Darnell grabbed Teboy's hand, pulling him off the porch. Darnell and Teboy walked toward the barn entrance.

Darnell hollered, "Dad told us to close and secure the barn floor door so no one can get back into the cave!"

Coley disappeared into the farmhouse, hollering for her dad. Mr. Morcort stepped out on the porch, surprised to see Tibby and Fogel.

Mr. Morcort asked, "What's going on, boys?"

Tibby started to speak, but Coley interrupted. "Dad, there are boys in the cave."

Mr. Morcort's face was showing anger as he looked at Tibby and Fogel, asking, "Did you boys tell your friends about the cave and the cave people?"

Fogel hollered, "They ain't our friends, and we haven't told anyone!"

Tibby stammered, "Mr. Morcort, Starber followed Kurpit, Jerk, and Mouse from the creek through the woods to the barn and down the steps to the cave. They have to be in the cave now."

Mr. Morcort jumped off the porch and ran to the barn entrance, hollering, "Darnell, Teboy! Don't close the floor door or secure it!"

Coley, Tibby, Fogel, and Starber followed Mr. Morcort into the barn. The floor door was closed, and Teboy was about to nail boards on the door to secure it. Mr. Morcort motioned the boys to step back, and he removed the boards, opening the floor door, and instructed Darnell to get a flashlight.

Fogel snickered. "Mr. Morcort, let's keep Kurpit, Jerk, and Mouse in the cave." Tibby and Fogel were laughing. Starber jumped on the steps, growling.

Mr. Morcort asked, "Are you sure those boys are in the cave?"

Starber continued growling on the stairs.

Tibby replied, "Starber is telling us that Kurpit and his friends are down in the cave."

Darnell returned with the flashlight, and Mr. Morcort announced, "You kids stay here, except Teboy. Teboy, you come with me."

Fogel spit on the barn floor, smiling, and replied, "Mr. Morcort, Tib, Roscoe, Starber, and I rescued your family from the cave people, remember?"

Mr. Morcort nodded his agreement, adding, "Fogel, you're right. Tibby, Fogel, come with us."

Darnell hollered, "Dad, we will need no-sees-um! The cave people will see us!"

Mr. Morcort replied, "We saw the cave people leave with King Daggerdash. They are on the way to Tura Land. You kids follow me and Teboy. We stay together. Darnell and Teboy will find the no-sees-um when we are in the cave."

Kurpit, Jer, and Mac were amazed at the waterfall and the colors flashing on the cave ceiling. Kurpit touched the water, hollering, "Jerk, Mouse, the water is warm! Let's go swimming!" The boys pitched off their shirts and pants. The three were swimming in the water, climbing the rock ledges, and jumping into the water.

Kurpit hollered, "Hey, Jerk, Mouse, watch me!" Kurpit jumped from a higher ledge, landing in the water. There was a loud screeching noise. The boys in the water looked around in the cave lake.

Then Kurpit, Jerk and Mouse saw a huge green something fly down the waterfall into the cave lake, with a huge splash.

The boys started screaming, "Sharks!" and swimming fast toward the rock ledge. Kurpit was raised out of the water, sitting on something moving fast. Kurpit was hollering and screaming. "Jerk, Mouse, help me! Don't let this shark eat me!"

Jer and Mac climbed on the ledge, scared to move, while watching Kurpit go under the water then return above, still hollering and screaming for help. He was splashing and sitting on something. Again there was a loud screeching noise and then a voice. "Darnell, is that you?"

Kurpit was still hollering for help. The strange voice

spoke. "You can't be Darnell, who is my friend. Who are you?"

Kurpit was now hollering, screaming, and crying while Jer and Mac, horrified, watched from the ledge.

The strange voice continued. "Don't be scared. I won't hurt you. My name is Roscoe. What's your name?"

Kurpit was screaming and crying when Roscoe pitched him on a rock ledge. Kurpit stood up, running toward Jer and Mac. Kurpit, crying, hollered, "Grab your clothes and run! This place is haunted!"

The boys ran to the barn stairs, almost knocking down Mr. Morcort. The loud screeching noise continued as Darnell hollered, "That's Roscoe!"

Mr. Morcort grabbed Kurpit's arm. Fogel grabbed Jer and Mac by their necks, holding them.

Mr. Morcort demanded, "What are you boys doing down here? You are trespassing on our property."

Fogel, holding Jer and Mac, forced them to the ground and looked at Kurpit, hollering, "Kurpit, you tried to set our tree house on fire, didn't you? Here's what your going to get for trying to burn up our tree house." Fogel shook both Jer and Mac, pulling them both up from the cave floor to the steps and shoving them from the steps to the floor. Fogel hollered, "Kurpit, I owe you my big fist!"

Mr. Morcort shook his head. Starber was barking and growling at Kurpit when Tibby spoke.

"Fogel, leave them alone. We will let the Village Police arrest them."

Jer and Mac started complaining and then shouted, "It was Kurpit's idea to set the tree house on fire! He wanted us to follow him to the barn and in the cave!"

Coley and Darnell, on the ledge by the cave lake, were talking to Roscoe. Mr. Morcort demanded, "You three boys put on your clothes now. Let's go; get your clothes on now. Darnell, Coley, we're leaving soon as these boys get their clothes on."

They were back in the barn. Teboy waved and was walking down the stairs toward the cave. He stopped and turned around, facing everyone. "Teboy return to cave to his people. Teboy will miss Darnell and his family. Teboy go now."

Darnell moaned, with tears dropping from his eyes, then hollered, "Teboy, please don't leave me! We are best friends!"

Coley hollered, "Teboy, stay here with us! You don't look like the cave people!"

Darnell shouted, "Teboy use the no-sees-um!"

They watched Teboy disappear down the stairs.

Mr. Morcort dropped the barn floor door. Kurpit, Jer, and Mac ran from the barn to the bridge to get their bikes. Tibby, Fogel, and Starber chased them. Kurpit picked up his bike, jumping on it, but Fogel grabbed the bike seat and pushed the bike to the bridge floor.

Fogel grabbed Kurpit, about to smash Kurpit's face with his fist, when Tibby shouted, "Fogel, stop it! Let's all sit down here and talk!"

Fogel motioned for Kurpit, Jer, and Mac to sit. Starber looked at them, growling. Tibby spoke. "Why, Kurpit, did you want to destroy our tree house? What have we done to you guys?"

Kurpit stammered, "Fogel was our friend, and you took him from us."

Fogel hollered, "That ain't true, Kurpit! Tibby and Rex never took me from you guys. I left you guys. I am lucky they are my friends, the way you and I use to bully them."

Tibby, shaking his head, smiling, announced, "Come on, guys; let's all be friends." Tibby raised his hand.

Fogel was shaking his head, saying, "Tib, are you sure you want to do this?" Fogel slowly raised his hand, joining Tibby. Tibby motioned for Kurpit, Jer, and Mac to join.

Tibby and Fogel chanted, "True friends together, always." All hands were locked together as once again everyone chanted, "True friends together, always."

Fogel raised his right fist at Kurpit, explaining, "You, Jerk, and Mouse are now our friends. You guys keep quiet and never tell anyone about the Morcorts' cave, Teboy, or Roscoe. Do you guys understand?"

Kurpit Jer, and Mac nodded, chanting, "Yes, Fogel."

Tibby replied, "Now we are friends. Come on; let's go to our tree house so you guys can meet Rex." Starber barked his approval. waging his tail. The boys rode their bikes back to the village and dropped them in Rex's backyard.

Fogel grabbed Kurpit, raising his fist. "That's our tree house that you, Jerk, and Mouse tried to destroy."

Tibby replied, "Yeah, and we still have mud balls stuck inside and outside of our tree house. I tried to remove the mud balls earlier with the water hose, but it made a mess. You guys clean the mud off the tree house and maybe we will forget how you tried to destroy it with fire."

Fogel demanded, "You, Jerk, and Mouse can clean the mud off our tree house. Get busy now before I put bumps on your faces." Fogel raised both fists. "Over there is the water hose. Now you guys get busy and clean all that mud from the outside and the inside of our tree house!"

Rex was in his house and heard Fogel hollering. Looking out the window, he saw Kurpit and his friends spraying their tree house. Rex left the house, carrying a mop bucket containing rags, and placed it by the tree. Rex returned to his garage and hollered, "Hey, guys, help me carry this ladder!"

Fogel hollered from the tree house. "Kurpit, Jerk, and Mouse, help Rex carry that ladder! You need to clean the mud balls! Go now before I climb down from this tree house and give you guys a payback!"

Kurpit hollered, "Stay there, Fogel!" Fogel laughed watching Kurpit carry the ladder. Rex climbed the tree ladder and joined Tibby and Fogel in their tree house.

Tibby whispered, "Rex, when they are done cleaning our tree house, we are going to allow them to be our friends. They will be able to come inside our tree house."

Rex moaned, "TB, you got to be kidding me."

Tibby said, "Come on, guys; let's agree."

Fogel replied, "Yeah, when the three are done cleaning our tree house."

Tibby laid back against the wall, shaking his head and looking at Fogel and Rex. "Guys, we still haven't found Elock."

Rex replied, "TB, you got to be kidding me."

Teboy, back in the cave, was walking on the rock ledges by the cave lake, looking for crevices to find the no-sees-um. There was a loud terrible screeching noise and then a splash. Teboy was aware of Roscoe. He had watched Darnell and Coley ride and talk to the big fish with wings.

Roscoe, splashing the water, approached Teboy near the ledge. "Teboy, is Darnell with you? Someone was in the lake riding me and kept hollering, screaming, and crying. I didn't do anything to him. I tried to talk to him. I know it wasn't Darnell or Coley. They have never been scared of me."

Teboy looked at Roscoe, replying, "Not Darnell. Another earthling."

Roscoe splashed the water, asking, "Where is Darnell?"

Teboy replied, "I'm looking for no-sees-um. Darnell is back on earth with Coley and family. Teboy find my family at Tura Land."

After more screeching and splashing, Roscoe asked, "Teboy go to Tura Land? My home too. Cave people caught me in net. Brought me here to grow and eat. The falls, this lake, Coley, Tibby, Fogel, and Starber have saved me. Teboy, can you get me back to Tura Land, to my home?"

Teboy, sitting on the ledge and looking at Roscoe, replied, "Roscoe, you good friend. Teboy never eat Roscoe or let anyone eat you. Maybe the king's friend Elock can take you to Tura Land."

Roscoe made his screeching noise, splashing the water, and said, "Teboy look like Darnell."

Teboy jumped on the rock ledges, checking the cracks for no-sees-um. Teboy hollered, "Must find no-sees-um!"

❋

Tibby jumped up, hollering, "Guys, Roscoe told us he wants to go home to Tura Land! Maybe Teboy, or if we find Elock with his machine, could help. We have to get back in the cave."

Rex stammered, "TB, you got to be kidding me. You always tell me Elock was just a crazy dream. Why go back in the cave?"

Tibby nodded. "You're right, Rex. It was a dream, but so was Coley and Darnell Morcort, who are real. Elock could be real."

Fogel bragged, "Tib, I ain't scared. Let's go."

Tibby replied, "We have one big problem with Kurpit, Jerk, and Mouse, who are still cleaning our tree house. What are we going to do about those guys?"

Rex continued. "You got to be kidding me."

Tibby whispered, "I was laying here thinking about Darnell playing with toys on his porch. Remember, he told us the toys were Elock and what looks-like-a-brown-bean machine. Darnell told us he and Teboy took the toys from King Daggerdash's son, Little Dash. Our camp and tent are still on the ledge by the river. We know how to find the no-sees-um in the cave. Roscoe told us the cave people brought him from his home in Tura Land to grow and eat. Teboy may know how to contact Elock. I should have asked him when we were with him at the Morcorts. Are you guys going with me?"

Fogel whispered, "Hey, guys, I've been watching Kurpit, Jerk, and Mouse. They are done cleaning the outside of the tree house. Here they come, climbing the tree ladder to clean the mud inside. Let me handle this."

Fogel opened the trap door, and Kurpit was about to get inside, with Jer and Mac hanging behind him on the tree ladder. Fogel grabbed Kurpit, explaining to him, "You guys have to pass our test for club membership before you can come inside to clean and we can accept you in our club. The test will start at dawn. You must be here. You can't tell anyone about Morcorts' cave, cave lake, Roscoe, or Teboy. Is that understood?"

Kurpit nodded his head, ordering, "Jerk and Mouse, climb down the ladder." The boys were off the ladder on the ground as Kurpit told them, "We have to take a test for club membership and clean the tree house inside. We are to return to the tree house at dawn." Starber barked, getting up from the ground by the tree.

Tibby, Fogel, and Rex watched Kurpit, Jer, and Mac leave Rex's backyard on their bikes. Fogel was laughing as Rex asked, "Fogel, what tests?"

Fogel replied, looking at Rex, "No tests, and when they show up at dawn, no one will be here. I didn't say which dawn. We keep them guessing, which gives us the time to find Elock."

Tibby replied, "Fogel, you are great."

Rex nodded his head, replying, "You got to be kidding me."

Tibby raised his hand as Fogel and Rex joined hands, all chanting, "True friends together, always."

The cave people, with King Daggerdash, had stopped to rest on their trip to Tura Land. One of the guards approached the king, reporting, "Ym Taerg Gnik, ew evah owt fo ruo elpoep gnissim. S'ti Teboy dna Rocklene." (My

125

Great King, we have two of our people missing. It's Teboy and Rocklene.) "Eht seilmaf era gniveirg." (The families are grieving.) "Yeht eveileb rieht sdik llef otni sa erif tip elihw gnilevart ot Arut Dnal." (They believe their kids fell into a fire pit while traveling to Tura Land.)

The king replied, "Gnirb eht stnerap ot em." (Bring the parents to me.) Teboy's parents were brought by several guards, and bowed before King Daggerdash.

Teboy's dad was several inches taller than Teboy. Rocklene's dad was shorter. Their faces were covered with whiskers. They had long braided hair, were in bare feet, extending on both sides of their shoulders, and an animal hide covered their bodies. Teboy's mother and Rocklene's mother had wrinkled skin and long hair and were tall, thin, and in bare feet. Their bodies were covered with an animal skin. Teboy's parents and Rocklene's parents bowed, chanting, "Ho, ym Taerg Gnik, ew evah tsol Teboy dna ruo Rocklene." (Oh my Great King, we have lost Teboy and our Rocklene.)

The king's son, Little Dash, hollered, "Teboy saw syawla htiw Darnell eht gnilhtrae." (Teboy was always with Darnell the earthling.)

The king raised his arms and hands above his head. "Ho, Taerg Tirips, reah em, sa ew evah tsol Teboy dna

Rocklene." (Oh Great Spirit, hear me, as we have lost Teboy and Rocklene.) "Esaelp erac rof eht stnerap." (Please care for the parents.) "Elpoep eb efas." (People be safe.) "Ew levart no ot Tura Land." (We travel on to Tura Land.)

Village Police Officer Sergeant Jill was with Professor Quizzley in the police interview room. Police officers had brought Professor Quizzley's brother, Brent Quizzley, the owner of the Village Bank, into the interview room. Brent was older, shorter, and heavier than the professor. Police Chief Boyd walked into the room, ordering Brent Quizzley to be moved to another room. Sergeant Jill and several police officers removed Brent.

Chief Boyd started asking questions. "Professor Quizzley, was this your idea or your brother's idea to scare people about a volcano eruption so you could find gold?"

The professor asked, "Eh, Chief, don't you have to advise me of my rights? Soon as you do, I want to contact my attorney."

Chief Boyd smiled and left the interview room, entering the other room with the professor's brother, Brent Quizzley. Chief Boyd requested the sergeant and officers to leave the room and asked Brent the same question.

Brent, smiling, said, "Chief Boyd, we have known each other for a long time. You know I have a reputation in the village and own my bank. Why would I want to ruin my reputation? My younger brother, the professor, was bound and determined to find gold. I had shown him a gold nugget I keep in my safe that I had received from old man Morcort to keep the paperboy paid each week. I have been sending the money and a nice tip in the mail to the paperboy. I told my brother that there could be gold in the creek at Morcorts' farm. I had no idea my brother was going to lie about a volcano eruption to scare people from the area so he could find gold. Chief Boyd, I hope you understand I own the bank, deal with the village people, and I have to keep my reputation. Can I see my brother now and return to my bank?"

Chief Boyd, smiling, motioned for Brent to follow him as they left the room and entered the interview room with his younger brother, Professor Dan Quizzley, sitting at a table with a microphone and recorder. Brent sat in a chair beside his brother. Chief Boyd advised the professor of his legal rights. "Professor Quizzley, before I ask you any questions you must understand your rights. You have the right to remain silent. Anything you say can be used in court. You have the right to talk to a lawyer before I ask you any questions and to have him with you during questioning. If you cannot afford a lawyer one will be appointed for you before questioning if you wish. If you decide to answer my questions now without a lawyer present you have the right to stop questions at any time until you talk to a lawyer. Do you understand what I have read to you? Knowing these rights do you wish to talk to me now?"

Professor Quizzley answered, "Yes," nodding his head, and continued. "Chief, I want to contact my attorney."

Brent Quizzley jumped up from his chair, hollering, "Brother, stop this crazy nonsense now! You know I own the village bank and have a reputation, which you are about to destroy!"

The professor repeated, "I want an attorney."

Brent Quizzley hollered, "Brother, I wish I had never shown you that gold nugget in my safe. It's made you crazy with nonsense falsely telling everyone about a volcano about to erupt. You were scaring people so you could find gold. You're a college professor with a reputation. Stop this nonsense that you want an attorney and think about your students and your school."

Professor Quizzley stood up, quivering, tears flowing from his eyes as he spoke. "Chief Boyd, I am sorry. I really thought we could find gold to help finance our university and students who want to come to our university. The economy is slow, and I wanted to help these students who don't have the funds to attend our university. I was believing the gold would be our answer. I am so sorry that I have scared people. I didn't want them finding the gold before me and my students."

Chief Boyd smiled and unlocked the handcuffs on the professor. "Brent, take your brother to the university, and you go back to your bank. I will talk to the mayor and Governor Turnmiester. If they agree I will drop the charges on your brother. Go on; get out of here."

A DISCOVERY

Teboy walked back into the cave tunnel, past the Great Fountain and, hearing the steam, stopped and tried to decide if he wanted to ride the steam out of the cave to live with the Morcorts.

He stood at the fountain, waiting for the noise and steam. Hearing it, he started to leap forward but stopped, almost falling into the fountain. He whispered, "No, Teboy have to find king, Dad, Mom, people, and Elock. Teboy get Roscoe back to Tura Land." Teboy walked away from the fountain, because he's alone. he climbs on the rock ledges looking for no-sees-um in the rock crevices to protect him from the vicious hide-beings and wing-beings in the cave.

Mr. Tearman had told his son, Rex, no more camping at the creek with Tibby, Fogel, and Starber. Rex was sad because he was not with his friends, but he really didn't want to return to the cave.

Tibby, Fogel, and Starber were at the tent on the ledge by the creek. Tibby grabbed Fogel, pulling him away from the tent and down the rock ledges toward the creek. Tibby stood on the bank and began the loud screeching noise.

Starber was barking, and Fogel hollered, "Hey, Tib, you calling Roscoe?" Tibby nodded, making the noise. Starber barked and ran along the creek path.

Starber stopped, whining and wagging his tail. Fogel hollered, "Tib, Starber has found Roscoe!" There was that loud screeching noise and a splash by the path where Starber was standing.

Roscoe said, "Hi, Tibby, Fogel, and Starber. Where are Darnell and Coley?"

Tibby stood on the path. "Roscoe, we need your help to fly us down the waterfall into the cave."

Fogel said, "Yeah, Roscoe, we want to find Elock."

Roscoe continued screeching and splashing the water with his wing, replying, "Tibby, Fogel, I talked to Teboy, who told me he was going to look for Elock to take me to Tura Land."

Tibby jumped and danced around the path, hollering, "Fogel, I told you and Rex that Elock was in my dream and might be real! Coley and Darnell Morcort are real!" Tibby continued, talking to Roscoe. "I knew when Darnell was playing with the two toys on the porch at the farmhouse, calling them Elock and Elock's machine, my dream could be real."

Roscoe screeched and slapped the water with his wing, replying, "Tibby, Fogel, I hope Elock is real. I want to go to my family at Tura Land. If you want to ride on me down the waterfall into the cave, hop on and hold on to my wings." Starber didn't wait for Tibby's command, jumping from the path onto Roscoe. Tibby and Fogel sat on Roscoe's back, holding on to his top wing. Tibby held Starber by his collar as Roscoe swam in the creek toward the creek's entrance to the cave and flew down the waterfall into the cave lake.

Fogel was hollering, "Yeah, Tib, Starber, this is great! It's like riding on a roller coaster, only I couldn't raise my hands above my head!"

The boys and Starber jumped off Roscoe onto a rock

ledge. Roscoe screeched and slapped the water. "Tibby, Fogel, and Starber, if you need me, make my noise. I will stay in the cave lake area. Please find Elock."

Tibby replied, "Thanks, Roscoe. We will find Teboy and try to find Elock." Tibby, Fogel, and Starber were wet from riding on Roscoe. Tibby whispered, "Come on, Fogel; we will soon be dry when we get into the warm tunnel and walk down the rock steps to the Great Fountain."

Fogel tapped Tibby, asking, "Hey, Tib, should we holler for Teboy? The cave people are gone."

Tibby replied, "Fogel, we saw them leave for Tura Land but maybe some have returned. We better be quiet and whisper when we talk."

Fogel patted the gold sparkling rocks around the fountain while talking. "You beautiful rocks, don't you go anywhere, because we want to keep you in our tree house."

Tibby laughed, and Starber barked. Tibby and Fogel followed Starber, leaving the fountain and heading toward the lighted path. They continued down the path, arriving at the platform and the tunnel entrance to King Daggerdash's room.

Walking inside, Fogel whispered, "Tib, the two gold chairs are gone."

Tibby replied, "Remember? We saw the king's guards carry the chairs when they went to Tura Land."

Fogel sighed. "Those chairs would have been great in our tree house." The boys looked around the king's room, and Fogel jumped on the king's leaf bed and, laying down, announced, "I am the king! Off with his head!" Starber barked, and both boys were laughing when something grabbed Tibby's arm.

Tibby was hollering, and Starber was growling. Fogel jumped from the king's bed, raising his fists and striking blows in the air as Tibby was being pulled away from Fogel and forced to sit on the cave floor.

Fogel was about ready to leap in the air and make a tackle when they heard, "Fogel, Tibby, and Starber, it's me, Teboy. You no see me. Have on no-sees-um. Why you here? Very dangerous here."

Tibby stood up, replying, "We were looking for you, Teboy. Can you help us find Elock? We promised Roscoe we would get him back to Tura Land with his family."

Teboy replied, "Teboy help Roscoe go to Tura Land. You follow Teboy. We look for no-sees-um for Tibby, Fogel, and Starber. Teboy help look for Elock."

Tibby, forgetting to whisper, shouted, "Teboy, there really is an Elock?"

Fogel chimed in, "Tib, you got to be kidding me."

Tibby moaned, "Fogel, you sound like Rex."

Teboy continued speaking. "I hear cave people talk about Elock. Elock look different. Elock no hear, no ears, talk in head. Elock give toys to Little Dash. King's friend is Elock."

Tibby asked, "Teboy, where is Elock? Does Elock have what looks-like-a-brown-bean machine? Have you ever seen Elock?"

Teboy shook his head no, replying, "Tibby, Fogel, and Starber find no-sees-um."

Upon checking several crevices in rock ledges, enough no-sees-um goop was found, and Tibby, Fogel, and Starber were invisible like Teboy.

Teboy commanded, "Tibby, Fogel, grab hands, stay together." The boys hung on to Teboy. Tibby held on to Starber with a small rope he had tied on Starber's collar before they had left the king's room. The boys started walking on the rock ledges, following Starber downward into the cave. Teboy whispered, "Stay together, very dangerous." The lights from the earth fires would dim then get brighter. The boys and Starber walked around the fire pits, which contained leaping fires. The smell of sulfur was strong. Tibby held the rope with one hand while holding on to Teboy. Fogel was holding on to Tibby. They climbed or jumped on the rock ledges.

Tibby and Fogel were surprised how Teboy maneuvered around the rock ledges in the dark areas. They continued walking on the ledges farther downward into the earth. Something furry touched Fogel, and he yelled. "Tib, something's got my leg!"

Teboy responded, "Teboy leave; stay here." The boys heard a yelp, and Starber was biting at the rope, trying to get loose, and growling. Teboy, snickering, said, "All okay. Teboy kick furry rat no-sees-um trying to bite Fogel. Tibby grab me. Fogel grab Tibby."

The boys continued walking down the ledges in the darkness. Teboy stopped on a ledge, whispering, "We stop here. We rest now." Starber was trying to move away, but Tibby pulled on the rope until Starber was standing beside him. Tibby sat down, placing Starber between his legs. Tibby whispered, "Fogel, are you okay?"

Fogel tapped Tibby, replying in a whisper, "I'm okay."

Tibby whispered, "Teboy, where is Tura Land?"

Teboy replied, "Much farther. We rest now."

It was dawn, and Kurpit, with his friends Jer and Mac, climbed the ladder on the walnut tree to the tree house in Rex's backyard. Kurpit knocked on the tree house door, expecting Tibby, Fogel, or Rex to open it. Kurpit hollered, looking down at Jer and Mac behind him, "Their ain't nobody here! Fogel told us to meet here at dawn!"

Rex's bedroom window faced the backyard, and he heard Kurpit hollering. Rex tiptoed to the back door so as not to awake his parents. He opened the door just as Kurpit was about to push on the doorbell. Rex whispered, "Kurpit, what are you, Jerk, and Mouse doing here this early?"

Kurpit shook his head, pointing toward the tree house, and asked, "Where are Fogel and Tibby? We were supposed to be here at dawn."

Jer and Mac started talking at the same time. "Yeah, man, we're getting the shaft from Fogel and the goofball."

Kurpit tapped Jer, commanding, "Jerk, Mouse, shut up, knock it off, before I knock you both to the ground." Kurpit, looking at Rex, asked, "Rex, where are Fogel and Tibby? Why aren't you in the tree house? What's going on?"

Rex smiled, replying, "I heard Fogel tell you to be here at dawn Monday, not today. This is Saturday."

Kurpit looked at Jer and Mac. "Hey, guys, we goofed.

We are supposed to be here Monday at dawn. Sorry, Rex, and I hope we didn't wake your parents."

Rex watched as Kurpit, Jer, and Mac hopped on their bikes and disappeared from his backyard. Rex grinned, closing the door, and returned to his bedroom. He couldn't wait to tell TB and Fogel how he had handled Kurpit, Jer, and Mac.

❋

Teboy shook Tibby, then Fogel, waking both. "Come, get up; we now go to Tura Land."

Tibby was still holding Starber by his collar and rope but jumping up, he let go, and Starber was loose. Starber was loose, invisible, and growling, and then Tibby heard a yelp. Tibby was scared thinking something happened to Starber.

Teboy said, "Starber protected us from a no-sees-um. No-sees-um would bite us."

Fogel chimed in, "Yeah, one tried to eat my leg."

Tibby shouted, "Starber, come here! Good boy, Starber." Starber was jumping on Tibby's leg. Tibby found and grabbed the rope, announcing, "I have Starber." The three boys, with Starber, continued walking down the rock ledges into the dark earth.

Fogel stopped, whispering, "Tib, Teboy, do you hear that? It sounds like running water below us."

Tibby could see Fogel's face as they moved close to the leaping fire pits in the rocks. Tibby pulled on Teboy's arm, whispering, "Teboy, I can see your and Fogel's faces."

Fogel answered, "Guys, I am sweating from this heat, and it's washing no-sees-um from me. Tibby and Teboy, I can see you and now Starber. You have been sweating from this heat."

Starber was panting, now wet around his mouth, which was visible.

Tibby, concerned, commanded, "Guys, we have to get more no-sees-um, or the cave people will see us. We are going to have to remove some of our clothes to keep from sweating."

Teboy started walking away from Tibby, Fogel, and Starber. "Teboy find more no-sees-um. Tibby, Fogel, Starber, wait here. Teboy will come back. Teboy get more no-sees-um."

Fogel and Tibby sat on the rock ledge with enough light to see each other and Starber. Tibby held Starber by the rope and collar, placing Starber between his legs as he sat down.

Fogel whispered, "Tib, nobody better mess with us. I

am going to move this huge rock so I can lay down." Fogel pushed and grunted as the rock moved, rolling off the ledge and crashing into other rocks, causing them to roll down until there was a splash.

Tibby whispered, "Fogel, did you hear the splash? You're right; there is water below us, and maybe it's flowing from the cave lake." Tibby was excited and jumped up and down on the ledge, and Starber was barking. "Fogel, we will get Roscoe to his family if the water below us flows to Tura Land."

Fogel, nodding, jumped up and down on the ledge, excited. The ledge began to move, and Fogel grabbed Tibby, who was holding Starber. Fogel jumped to another ledge, pulling Tibby and Starber with him as the earth around them shook. They landed down on a ledge and could hear water moving below.

Tibby spoke. "Fogel, I hope Teboy is okay. We need to see if this water will take us to the cave lake or Tura Land."

Fogel asked, "What do you suggest?"

Tibby pointed below at the moving water and replied, "Let's check out this water and see where it goes. We may be able to follow it back to the cave lake to get Roscoe. Right now we have to climb up on the ledge where Teboy left us so he can find us. He will be looking for us."

Tibby pointed to the ledges above and whispered, "Starber will show us how to get back up there." Starber barked and started leaping to higher ledges. Tibby held tight to the rope, and the boys followed Starber, climbing on each ledge higher in darkness, but they could see fires seeping from the earth on higher ledges. They arrived on the rock ledge higher than where Fogel had moved that big rock that caused other rocks to fall into the water below. Starber jumped on Tibby, and both boys thanked Starber. The boys sat down on the ledge, waiting for Teboy to return.

It was Sunday morning, and church was over. Tibby's dad was tall and thin, with short blond hair and glasses. His mom was tall and thin, with long red hair, and was very attractive. They left the church and decided to go to the bridge over the creek to find Tibby and his friends' camp and to see if the boys were okay.

Arriving at the bridge, they recognized Tibby and Fogel's bikes. Parking their car, they could see the boys' tent on the ledge above the creek. Tibby's dad and mom walked from the bridge and down the creek bank and climbed up the rock ledge to the boys' tent to surprise them. They entered the tent, finding the black Halloween hair.

Tibby's mom picked up some dark Halloween hair, asking, "What in the world would our son and his friends be doing with this?"

Tibby's dad picked up several feed bags, laughing, and said, "The boys are using these bags to carry the fish home they are catching." They left the tent and looked up and down the creek, hoping to see the boys fishing. "I guess Tibby and his friends are farther down the creek fishing, so we should return home. The boys will be coming back to the village on Monday. Let's go, and be careful climbing down this rock ledge."

Mr. Brawlien grabbed his wife's hand, helping her down the ledges to the creek and bridge.

Teboy returned and was looking for Tibby, Fogel, and Starber, who were sitting on a higher ledge. Starber was growling.

Tibby and Fogel stood up in the dim light, looking down and around and listening. Starber continued growling when something tapped Tibby on the shoulder with a whisper. "Teboy come back. Hear Starber. Teboy has more no-sees-um for Tibby, Fogel, and Starber."

Teboy handed the goop to Tibby and Fogel, who

smeared more over their faces. Tibby placed goop on Starber's mouth and in his pocket, telling Fogel, "Hey, Fogel, if you have extra goop, put it in your pocket. Teboy, thanks for no-sees-um. Fogel and I found water moving below us that might be from the cave lake. If we follow the water, it could take us to the cave lake or Tura Land. Roscoe could use this moving water to swim to Tura Land and be with his family."

Fogel said, "Tib, I'm with you. How about you, Teboy?"

Teboy, holding the boys' hands and raising them, said, "Teboy true friends together, always."

Tibby held the rope to Starber's collar as the boys and Teboy moved over the ledges, heading downward to the moving water. As they continued downward, some ledges were smaller and more difficult to move on.

Teboy and the boys were surprised that the ledges were small. Tibby released the rope to make it easier for Starber to move. Starber jumped, missed a small ledge, and fell into the water below. Tibby moaned and cried out, "Guys, Starber fell below! I am going to join him!" Tibby pushed off from the ledge and, falling feet first, entered the water. Tibby hollered, "Guys, the water is warm, but it is moving fast. Hurry and join us."

Fogel, hanging on a ledge, heard the two splashes and

shouted, "Teboy, I'm going into the water with Tib and Starber!"

Teboy shouted, "Teboy join Tibby, Starber, and Fogel in water!" Teboy pushed from the ledge, falling into the water, missing Tibby, Starber, and Fogel, who were swimming. The water was warm, and Teboy and the boys were floating while Starber was swimming with the water, moving them somewhere. They spotted a ledge above the water. Swimming with the current pushing them toward the ledge, they grabbed on, helping each other climb out of the water. They pulled each other up on the ledge and removed their wet clothes and shoes while watching Starber shake the water from his fur.

Fogel was looking around in the dim light and saw a shiny substance above them layered in the rocks. Fogel whispered, "Guys, do you see the rocks in that ledge above us shining?"

Teboy stood up, climbing on the rocks to the ledge, and Fogel followed him. Both boys were on the ledge, and Teboy was checking out the shiny substance.

Teboy rubbed his hand over the shiny rocks, announcing, "Dlog, dlog, dlog!" (Gold, gold, gold!) "S'gnik dlog!" (King's gold.)

Fogel hollered, "Tib, Teboy says it's gold!"

Starber was barking, and Tibby hollered, "Now we will know where we left our clothes and shoes when we see the shining gold! Teboy, which way to the cave lake or Tura Land?"

Teboy answered, "Maybe water flow to Tura Land or cave lake. We swim now." The water current continued pushing them forward at a fast pace into a rock wall. Their swimming was stopped, but they could hear water rushing below the wall.

Tibby said, "Guys, do you hear this water? It might be moving under this rock wall. I will swim under it and see where the water goes." Tibby took a deep breath of air and disappeared. Starber was whining and trying to swim while being pushed against the wall. Fogel and Teboy continued to push away from the wall, only to be returned by the flowing water.

There was a splash, and Tibby surfaced. "Guys, it just takes seconds to swim under the wall, and we will be swimming in the cave lake."

Tibby grabbed Starber by the collar, and both disappeared. Teboy and Fogel followed Tibby, swimming under the wall and surfacing in the cave lake. Starber and the boys swam toward a rock ledge. Pulling each other up on the ledge out of the water, Tibby made that screeching noise to call Roscoe.

In the cave lake, Roscoe heard Tibby and swam toward their location. Starber was shaking water from his body. There was a huge splash, and the screeching noise.

Roscoe was surprised seeing Tibby, Fogel, Teboy, and Starber on the rock ledge. Roscoe asked, "Teboy, Tibby, Fogel, and Starber, what are you doing here? How did you get here?"

Tibby replied, "Roscoe, we have found where water is flowing to the cave lake under a rock wall. The water current moves you toward the wall, and we swam under it. If you swim under the wall, that water might take you to Tura Land."

Roscoe was slapping the water with his wing and screeching. Roscoe asked, "Tibby, can you take me to the wall? Roscoe swim to Tura Land to find family."

Tibby jumped on Roscoe. They swam to the wall. Roscoe returned Tibby to the ledge with Teboy, Fogel, and Starber. Roscoe slapped the water with his wings and made more screeching noises, then said, "Thank you." Roscoe dove under the water and disappeared.

Tibby, smiling, whispered, "Roscoe is on his way home to join his family." Starber barked to agree, then whined.

There was a splash and the terrible screeching noise as Roscoe returned, demanding, "Roscoe swim with Teboy, Tibby, Fogel, and Starber to Tura Land."

Tibby replied, "Roscoe, that water current is strong."

Roscoe replied, "Roscoe take you to Tura Land. Ride on Roscoe." Starber jumped on Roscoe, and the boys jumped on behind Starber. Roscoe swam toward the cave wall, demanding, "Grab my wings. Roscoe swim under wall."

UNWANTED VISITORS

Coley Morcort was walking from their barn. She saw several cars parked on the creek bridge, and people on their property and in the creek. Coley ran into the house, hollering, "Dad, Dad! Mom, where is Dad?"

Mr. Morcort was busy cleaning his father's special room that contained documents, books, broken blinds, spider webs, and a chalkboard, where Coley had taught Tibby and Rex the cave people's language.

Coley again hollered, "Dad, there are cars parked on

the bridge, and people are in the creek, on our property, and maybe panning for gold."

Mr. Morcort looked out the dirty window and saw several people walking on their property toward the boys' camp and tent. Several younger boys were looking at an opening in the rock ledge and watching the steam rising from the earth. Mr. Morcort was mad, believing that Tibby, Rex, or Fogel had told people about the cave, cave people, and gold.

Coley approached her dad, who was still looking at the cars and people from the dirty window. Mr. Morcort, seeing Coley enter the room, spoke. "I guess our secret about the cave, cave people, and gold was to big a secret for the boys to keep to themselves."

Coley replied, "Dad, Tibby, Rex, and Fogel wouldn't tell anyone our secret. Rex had to tell his dad and the Village Police about the volcano eruption, which brought the police to the cave. Chief Boyd, Tibby, Rex, and Fogel promised us they would keep our secret. They wouldn't tell."

Mr. Morcort raced down the stairs and out the door and almost knocked down Darnell, who was playing with his toys on the porch. Darnell started to follow his dad. Mr. Morcort hollered, "Darnell, you get back on the porch and you stay there!"

Darnell moaned, "Okay, Dad," and returned to the porch.

Mr. Morcort approached several young boys who had found the open tunnel to the cave. They were attempting to move the heavy rocks that Fogel had placed to cover the entrance. Mr. Morcort, showing an angry face, demanded, "What are you boys doing here? You are trespassing on our property. You need to leave now."

One boy replied, "Sorry, sir, we are students from Genoris University. We were here the other day with Professor Quizzley. We returned here at the creek looking for gold and noticed this opening with these huge rocks, which looks like a tunnel to a cave. We are just exploring, and we didn't realize that we are trespassing as there are no No Trespassing signs. We are sorry." The boys all together chanted, "We are sorry, sir."

The same boy, with short hair, a medium but tall build, wearing glasses and a beard, continued. "Sir, if we could remove these huge rocks, there might be a tunnel leading to a cave. Our class has been studying about caves in our state, and we might have one here. Would you like us to remove the rocks and explore the tunnel to determine if there is a cave?"

Mr. Morcort's angry facial expression disappeared with

a smile as he patted the boy on the shoulder. Mr. Morcort replied, "Son, my family has lived in that farmhouse and on this property many years. My father explored this opening. It is very dangerous. We were told never to crawl inside this opening because of a huge sinkhole. My father placed these huge rocks over the opening to keep our family safe."

The boys nodded, agreeing. "Sinkholes are dangerous. Thanks for stopping us from exploring this opening."

The boys waved at Mr. Morcort as they walked down the ledges to the creek. Mr. Morcort retuned to his house and called the Village Police.

"Village Police, can I help you?"

"This is Mr. Morcort, and I need to talk with Chief Boyd."

"One minute, Mr. Morcort, while I connect you."

"Hello, this is Chief Boyd."

"Chief, this is Mr. Morcort. We have many people in the creek panning for gold. We have some college kids who were trespassing on our property and found a tunnel entrance to our cave. I told the kids the tunnel is dangerous because of a sinkhole."

Chief Boyd asked, "Did they believe you and leave your property?"

"Yes, Chief Boyd. Do you have any suggestions to stop people from trespassing on our property?"

Chief Boyd replied, "Mr. Morcort, I would suggest a fence with No Trespassing signs. If the trespassing continues, call us and I will send some officers to help you. I have told the officers who were with us in the cave and saw Teboy and the gold not to talk to anyone about it, or they will lose their job."

"Thank you, Chief Boyd," replied Mr. Morcort. He looked at his wife, Coley, and Darnell and explained the need for a fence and No Trespassing signs.

Coley spoke. "Dad, I can make the signs. Tibby and Fogel are at their camp fishing. They could help us install a fence."

Mr. Morcort shook his head, saying, "Okay, Coley, go ask Tibby and Fogel to help us. I will go to the hardware store to get the fence and poles."

Coley and Darnell raced down to the creek, running along the creek bank and looking for Tibby, Fogel, and Starber. They stopped and watched several people panning in the creek for gold. Darnell picked up a large rock, about to throw it into the creek to make a splash, when Coley grabbed his hand and stopped him, hollering, "No, Darnell!"

Some of the people panning for gold in the creek had heard Coley holler and were looking at them. Coley whispered, "Darnell, wave at the people looking at us." Both waved at the people and continued walking to the camp and tent. Coley entered the tent. Nobody was there, and all their equipment was still there. She and Darnell ran farther along the creek bank looking for Tibby, Fogel, and Starber. No one was in the area, so Coley started doing a screeching noise to call Roscoe. They waited, and Coley continued the noise.

Darnell hollered, "Coley, Tibby, Fogel, Starber, and Roscoe are back in the cave with Teboy!"

Coley, trying to keep her composure, asked, "Darnell, how do you know they are in the cave?"

Darnell snickered. "Tibby and Fogel's bikes are still at the bridge. There not at the camp, tent, or fishing in the creek. Roscoe isn't in the creek. Coley, they have to be in the cave with Teboy and Roscoe."

Coley, with tears flowing from her eyes, ran toward the bridge and to their house. Darnell ran beside Coley, chanting, "Coley has a boyfriend."

Tibby, holding Starber by his collar with one hand

and holding on to Roscoe's wing with his other, looked at Fogel.

Teboy was holding on to Roscoe's wings when Roscoe screeched, shoutimg, "Hold on tight!" Roscoe shouted, "I will jump and fly against the water!" Roscoe would swim against the water current then leap into the air. Tibby could see the sparkling rocks in the dim light. "Guys, there's our ledge where we left our clothes and shoes. Roscoe, swim to that ledge with the sparkling rocks."

Roscoe screeched, replying, "Okay, Tibby."

The boys were back on the ledge putting on their clothes and shoes. They returned, climbing on Roscoe, who continued swimming and leaping high in the water.

Teboy hollered, "Roscoe, there is a hide-being drinking water ahead of us!"

Tibby and Fogel were amazed as they were seeing what looked to them like a large bear drinking water.

Teboy hollered, "Roscoe, fly high over hide-being! Hide-being eat us! Dangerous!"

Roscoe screeched, flying out of the water and above the hide-being. The hide-being jumped, trying to grab Roscoe, then continued drinking water. Roscoe screeched and hollered, "Roscoe tired from swimming against water. Roscoe stop now." Roscoe swam to a close ledge above the water, and the boys and Starber jumped from Roscoe onto the ledge.

Roscoe screeched. "We rest here now and continue to Tura Land."

Fogel asked, "Teboy, what is a hide-being? It looks like a bear." Starber barked, then started growling. The boys stood up on the ledge and in the dim light could see hide-beings.

Teboy whispered, "Hide-beings dangerous. Cave people hunt hide-beings for meat and hides. Teboy look for no-sees-um now. Roscoe stay underwater. Tibby, Fogel, and Starber find hiding place. Teboy return with no-sees-um."

Tibby held Starber's mouth closed, as Starber was trying to growl. Tibby whispered, "No, Starber, stay quiet."

Fogel noticed a hole in a rock ledge and whispered, "Tib, follow me. I see a hole we can hide in." The boys and Starber managed to climb into the hole. Tibby was shaking his head, wondering if the hide-beings would find them. They waited and waited for Teboy to return.

Fogel whispered, "Teboy, is that you touching my arm?"

Tibby crouched farther back into the opening, still holding Starber's mouth, who was attempting to growl. The boys heard, "Tibby, Fogel, and Starber, it's me, Teboy, with no-sees-um." Teboy handed the boys the goop, who put the goop on themselves and Starber. All were invisible.

Teboy announced, "We now be quiet and walk around the hide-beings."

✳

Coley raced into the house, hollering for her dad. Darnell was jumping up and down, hollering, "Tibby, Fogel, Starber, and Roscoe are in the cave with Teboy!"

Mr. Morcort shook his head, asking, "Coley and Darnell, are you certain that the boys are in the cave?"

Coley shook her head, tears flowing from her eyes, and replied, "Dad, I don't know. We can't find Tibby, Fogel, and Starber at the camp or fishing in the creek. Their bikes are still by the bridge."

Mr. Morcort looked at his wife, asking, "Should I call Chief Boyd? I would hate to bother him if the boys are fishing in the creek."

Darnell hollered, "Dad, at our barbecue, Tibby, Rex, and Fogel talked about going back into the cave with Roscoe's help to find the king's friend Elock."

Mr. Morcort looked at Coley, asking, "Honey, what do you think we should do? The cave and cave people can be dangerous."

Coley, now crying, replied, "Dad, please call Chief Boyd. He will know what to do."

Teboy placed his hand in the water, making a circular motion. Roscoe saw his hand and surfaced, looking for Teboy, about to screech. Teboy stopped the screeching noise by placing his now visible hand on Roscoe's mouth.

"Roscoe, it's me, Teboy. You can't see me, only my hand. We have on no-sees-um. We will need to leave you here to get by the hide-beings, who would eat us. You swim underwater and be careful. We will meet you later to swim on to Tura Land."

Teboy patted Roscoe with his visible hand, and Roscoe replied, "Teboy, Tibby, Fogel, and Starber, be careful. Roscoe find you." Roscoe dove under the water, and Teboy applied more no-sees-um to his hand. Tibby grabbed Starber, holding his mouth. The boys climbed to the second ledge, where there in front of them were several hide-beings.

One hide-being stood up in the air like he was smelling something. Several others stood up sniffing, and Teboy whispered, "Hang on to Teboy and run."

✳

Mr. Morcort again was talking to Chief Boyd. "Chief Boyd, I hate to bother you again, but we may have a real problem."

"What is the problem, Mr. Morcort? Do you have more trespassers?"

"Chief Boyd, we may have boys back in the cave."

"Mr. Morcort, I thought you fixed the entrances so no one could get back in the cave."

"Chief Boyd, you remember the fish with wings, Roscoe?"

"Oh yes, Mr. Morcort, I remember and still don't believe what I saw and heard. A fish talking. What is the connection with the boys and the fish?"

"Chief Boyd, our kids, Coley and Darnell, would ride on Roscoe in the cave lake and creek. We believe the boys rode Roscoe from their camp in the creek to the waterfall and down into the cave lake."

"Mr. Morcort, are you telling me we need to return to the cave to find the boys?"

"I believe so, Chief Boyd." Mr. Morcort hung up the phone, looking at his wife. Coley was still in tears, and

Darnell excitedly jumped up and down. "Chief Boyd and his officers are coming here."

Teboy, Tibby holding Starber, and Fogel were invisible to the hide-beings and ran along on higher ledges above them. One hide-being climbed up the ledges and rose up on his legs and sniffed. Several other hide-beings followed him.

Teboy shouted, "Tibby, Fogel, the hide-beings smell us! Run, and hang on to me!"

Tibby was running so fast hanging on to Teboy that Starber fell from his arms. Tibby cried out, "Guys, Starber is loose!" They heard barking and growling but couldn't see Starber. The hide-beings stopped climbing and stood still while the barking and growling continued. One hide-being let out a howl and jumped to lower ledges, followed by the others.

Tibby was crying, believing that the hide-beings had hurt Starber. Fogel and Teboy patted Tibby on the shoulders, chanting, "True friends together, always."

Tibby jumped for joy when he heard whining next to him. Tibby reached down, and Starber jumped on his arm. Tibby picked up Starber, hugging him and realizing that he

160

had scared the hide-beings and saved their lives. The boys and Starber began climbing down the rock ledges to the flowing water to find Roscoe. Starber turned around and was growling. The boys turned around, believing there would be a hide-being about to jump on them. There was nothing behind them, but Starber continued growling and then would whine.

Tibby shouted, "Guys, Starber has found something. We need to follow him!"

Starber was moving up on the ledges, and Tibby tried to stay with him by hanging on to the rope. There was an opening in the rocks, and Starber, growling and whining, ran toward the opening. Tibby, trying to keep up with Starber, dropped the rope, and Starber was loose.

Fogel caught up with Tibby, asking, "Tib, what is happening?"

Starber had entered the opening and was jumping on someone. Tibby, Fogel, and Teboy slowly entered the opening, amazed when they found a cave girl huddled in a dark corner moaning and crying. Starber was licking the girl's face, trying to tell her she was safe.

Stooping and smiling, Teboy gently spoke. "Rocklene, tahw era uoy gniod ereh?" (Rocklene, what are you doing here?)

"She can't see us with our no-sees-um on." Fogel left the entrance, climbed down the ledge, and jumped in the water. Fogel returned while Tibby and Teboy watched her. The girl, the same age as Fogel, was about his size, with long braided hair, was pretty, and wore a hide to cover her body. When she saw Fogel, she stood up and tried to run from the opening. Teboy, Tibby, and Starber, still invisible, held her.

Teboy whispered, "I know this girl. She is Little Dash's cousin, and King Daggerdash is her uncle. Hold her while I wash off in the water."

Teboy returned visible. The girl, was still trying to get away. Seeing Teboy she hollered, "Teboy, Teboy, pleh em, pleh em!" (Teboy, Teboy, Teboy, help me, help me!) Teboy stooped down, and the girl hugged him. The girl stopped crying and looked at Fogel, smiling.

Tibby spoke. "I guess Starber and I should wash. Come on, Starber." Teboy, Fogel, and Rocklene followed Tibby and Starber to the water. Fogel was embarrassed when the girl grabbed his hand and held it. They sat on a ledge, watching Tibby and Starber become visible. The girl stood up and walked toward Starber, who was shaking the water from his fur. The girl held Starber, and Starber kissed the girl.

Teboy sat next to the girl, asking, "Rocklene, yhw t'nera uoy htiw ruoy ylimaf?" (Why aren't you with your family?)

She continued petting Starber and replied, "Teboy, Si tog deracs nehw Si was eht hide-beings. (Teboy, I got scared when I saw the hide-beings.) "Si dih ni eht skcor erehw uoy dnuof em." (I hid in the rocks where you found me.)

Fogel surprised Tibby when he walked over to the girl, smiling and raising his hand. "Eurt sdneirf rehtegot, syawla." (True friends together, always.)

The girl walked over to Fogel and kissed him on his cheek. Tibby was laughing and jumping on the ledge. Fogel was trying to hide his face. Teboy was grinning, and Starber was barking.

Tibby asked Teboy, "Does the girl know how to get to Tura Land?"

Teboy answered, "We all ride on Roscoe, and he will take us to Tura Land."

Tibby spoke. "Teboy, ask Rocklene if she knows Elock."

Teboy stooped down, looking at Rocklene, and asked, "Rocklene, od uoy wonk na Elock?" (Rocklene, do you know an Elock?)

Rocklene smiled at Fogel and answered, "Si evah draeh klat tuoba Elock tub evah reven nees mih." (I have heard talk about Elock but have never seen him.) "Elpoep yas eh sah on srae." (People say he has no ears.) "Skaeps otni ruoy daeh." (Speaks into your head.)

Tibby was laughing and jumping around. Starber was jumping on Tibby and barking. Tibby announced, "From here we could ride Roscoe to Tura Land." Tibby started screeching to call Roscoe. Rocklene was sitting beside Fogel, holding his hand and smiling at him. There was a screeching noise. Starber wasn't barking but growling.

Tibby hollered, "That's not Roscoe!" Turning his head, he saw Starber pulling on the rope with his teeth and growling. The screeching continued and was getting closer. Teboy was standing, looking around in the dim light at the flowing water.

The screeching noise was louder and louder as Rocklene, holding Fogel's hand, shouted, "Teboy, s'ti sa gniw-gnieb!" (Teboy, it's a wing-being!)

Teboy shouted, "Rocklene, teg ni eht retaw!" (Rocklene, get in the water!) Tibby, Fogel, Starber, get in the water!" Before Fogel could ask why, Rocklene, still holding his hand, jumped off the ledge, pulling Fogel into the water with her. The screeching was close, and Tibby could see several huge wing-beings flying above them.

Teboy shouted, "Rocklene, evid rednu eht retaw won!

(Rocklene, dive under the water now!) Tibby, Fogel, Starber, dive under the water now!"

Tibby grabbed Starber by the collar as he saw the flying wing-beings dive toward them, making a loud screeching noise. The boys, Rocklene, and Starber surfaced and quickly dove under the water several times. They would surface, and the flying wing-beings would dive at them. The flowing water current continued pushing them. Once again Teboy, Rocklene, Fogel, Tibby, and Starber surfaced, not seeing the creatures or hearing the screeching noise. The flowing water carried them to a rock ledge where they worked to pull each other out of the water.

They sat on the flat ledge, and Fogel asked, "What is a wing-being?"

Teboy, standing and looking around in the dim light, whispered, "Wing-beings very dangerous. Wing-beings scared of water. Wing-beings carry cave people away. Never see cave people again."

Tibby moaned, saying, "Teboy, you and Rocklene go on to Tura Land with Roscoe. I, Fogel, and Starber will return to the cave lake."

Rocklene stood, walking with Fogel and holding his hand. Teboy whispered, "Rocklene doesn't want to leave Fogel."

Fogel replied, "Teboy, do the wing-beings take the cave people to their nests and eat them? You live in this cave with hide-beings that will eat you, and now we jump in the water so wing-beings won't eat us. Hey, Tib, this is some place."

Tibby shook his head, and Starber barked while shaking the water from his fur. Tibby asked, "Teboy, did the wing-beings come here because I was calling Roscoe?"

Teboy replied, "We be quiet now. We watch flowing water to see Roscoe." They sat on the ledge, waiting for Roscoe.

Fogel asked, "Tib, do you still want to go to Tura Land?"

Tibby lowered his head, disgusted, tears welling up in his eyes, and shook his head.

Darnell was on the porch, playing with toys, when he saw several police cars moving over the creek bridge and up their path. Darnell jumped up, opened the front door, and hollered, "Dad, Mom, Coley, the police are here!"

Mr. Morcort walked outside and shook hands with Police Chief Boyd and the officers.

Chief Boyd, shaking his head, asked, "Mr. Morcort, do

you believe that Roscoe hauled two boys from their camp, carrying them into the cave lake below us?"

Before the chief could continue speaking, Darnell hollered, "I and Coley rode Roscoe in our cave lake and creek. I taught Roscoe how to talk." Several police officers stood shaking their heads and laughing.

Chief Boyd, looking angry, replied in a stern voice. "You guys laugh but notice the chief isn't laughing because I saw and talked to this Roscoe, a fish with wings. You guys want to continue to laugh?"

Mr. Morcort, who wasn't laughing, announced, "Guys, what the chief is telling you is true. Both of my children are friends with this fish, and they did ride him in the cave lake and creek. The fish also talks to us."

Coley and Darnell, standing by their dad, chimed in. "It's true." Several of the officers were telling the other officers about the cave lake, cave people, gold, and a cave man called Teboy.

Chief Boyd, with his officers, walked with Mr. Morcort, Coley, and Darnell to the barn. Officers turned on their flashlights as they slowly walked down the stairs to the cave. Several officers were talking to the others, telling them, "Wait till we get to the bottom of these stairs and you see a waterfall and various colors on the cave walls and the ceiling. If you believe that's incredible, wait until you see the Great Fountain surrounded by gold nuggets."

Chief Boyd turned to the officers talking, and whispered, "People, let's whisper because we may have cave people down here and they can hear you."

They reached the cave, and there were whispers about the beauty. Darnell left them, running toward the cave lake and making a loud screeching noise.

Mr. Morcort spoke. "Our son is calling Roscoe." Darnell continued the noise, and Coley stood beside her brother, making the same noise. Mr. Morcort, Chief Boyd, and his officers stood at the ledge by the lake.

Darnell whispered to Coley, "I guess Roscoe is somewhere below in the water and can't hear us. I will have to screech under the water." Darnell removed his shoes and dived into the water, screeching.

❉

Roscoe was swimming under the water to avoid the hide-beings and would surface looking for Teboy, Tibby, Fogel, and Starber. Roscoe heard Darnell's screeching underwater and stopped his swimming. Roscoe was listening and hearing the screeching noise. He knew it had to be Darnell making that noise. Roscoe turned around, swimming under the water, under the huge rock wall, and back in the cave lake.

Mr. Morcort motioned to Coley to get Darnell. Darnell was still screeching under the water. Darnell surfaced riding on something. Coley jumped up and down. Several police officers were pointing their guns and moving backward toward the stairs leading to the barn.

Darnell hollered, "It's okay. I am riding Roscoe." Several times Darnell submerged then would surface, laughing. Roscoe pitched Darnell up on the ledge, splashed, and screeched. Several officers plugged their ears.

Roscoe spoke. "Darnell and Coley, are you okay? I was swimming in the water. Tibby found how to get me to Tura Land. I had to swim underwater because of the hide-beings who would eat me. I heard Darnell screeching, so here I am. Darnell and Coley, are you okay?"

Several officers shined their lights at the big fish with wings. Roscoe asked, "Darnell, who is with you? Teboy, Tibby, Fogel, and Starber were riding me to take them to

Tura Land. We saw several huge hide-beings who would eat us. They left me with no-sees-um on and told me to look for them later."

Darnell, jumping up and down, looked at Coley, bragging. "See? I told you Tibby, Fogel, and Starber were with Teboy in the cave, looking for Elock."

The officers were laughing and talking. "Do you believe this? We are watching a big fish with wings talking to two kids."

Chief Boyd demanded, "People, what you see and hear stays here, is that clear? Telling anyone about what you are seeing or hearing will cost you your job, understood?"

The officers spoke together. "Yes, sir."

Coley walked over to her dad, shaking and crying. "Dad, Roscoe told us that Tibby, Fogel, and Starber are with Teboy going to Tura Land to find Elock. They had on no-sees-um to get by a herd of hide-beings."

Chief Boyd asked, "What is a hide-being?"

Mr. Morcort shook his head, replying, "They are big, like bears, and will eat you. Cave people hunt them for meat and use their hides to cover their bodies. The hide-beings are dangerous. I hope the boys and their dog are okay."

Chief Boyd, smiling, asked, "Mr. Morcort, could Roscoe carry me and several officers to where he left the boys?"

Mr. Morcort looked at Coley. "Do you think Roscoe could carry the chief and several officers to find the boys?"

Coley ran to the ledge where Darnell was taking to Roscoe. She asked, "Roscoe, could you carry Chief Boyd, me, and several police officers to where you left Teboy, Tibby, Fogel, and Starber?"

Roscoe splashed the water with his wing, screeching, and replied, "Coley, I will try. The water current is strong."

Coley motioned for Chief Boyd. The chief picked two officers to ride with him on Roscoe.

Chief Boyd spoke. "People who are not going with me, follow Mr. Morcort farther into the cave."

Mr. Morcort motioned for Darnell and Coley. Coley was hanging on to Roscoe's wing with Chief Boyd and the two officers. Darnell was mad, jumping around while watching Coley riding on Roscoe with the police. Mr. Morcort was not happy and walked over, grabbing Darnell, who was hollering, "Dad, it ain't fair! Coley is riding Roscoe with the police!"

Mr. Morcort replied, "Son, they need Coley as their guide, and we need you as our guide."

GOVERNOR BEN TURNMIESTER

Genoris University is in Genority City, the General state capital. Professor Quizzley was lecturing to his summer students when another professor entered the classroom, approached Professor Quizzley, and whispered to the professor. Professor Quizzley excused himself, speaking to the students. "I am sorry, class, but you are excused, as Governor Turnmiester wants to talk to me."

The students left the classroom, and Professor Quizzley returned to his office and picked up the phone.

"Is this Professor Dan Quizzley?"

There was a pause, then "Professor Quizzley, I apologize for interrupting your summer class. I had received word from the Village Police about you reporting a possible volcano eruption in the village area. Later the Village Police contacted my office reporting that it was a fabrication because of gold in the area. The police reported you were responsible. Is that true, Professor Quizzley?"

The professor cleared his throat several times and meekly answered, "Governor, you know our economy is slow. There are many kids who want to study at our university but can't because of expenses. Some of my regular students wanted to help, and so I told several people about the volcano eruption so our students could find the gold before other people."

There was a pause, then Governor Turnmiester continued. "Professor Quizzley, how did you know there was gold in the village creek?"

The professor took a deep breath. "Sir, my brother received a large gold nugget from a Mr. Morcort who lived on the farm by the creek. I believed that gold nugget was from the creek, so I and my students went there looking for gold but never found any. I was arrested by the Village Police and later released. Sir, I am sorry I lied, telling people about a volcano eruption. I will resign from the university and you can put me in jail, but please don't arrest any students."

The professor, crying and shaking, heard, "Professor Quizzley, you should never resign, and you won't go to jail. We appreciate your concern about your students. You should not have lied about a volcano eruption. I, along with our state government, want to help you and the students who want to come to our Genoris University. I am sending to your university a grant for five million dollars to help you finance those students."

Professor Quizzley, trying to dry his tears with his hand while holding the phone, trembled, asking, "Governor, is this real?"

Governor Turnmiester replied, "This is real, and you can thank one of our state merchants who had helped by providing the funds for this grant. Just promise me, Professor, no more lying about a volcano eruption."

The professor, smiling and jumping around his desk, replied, "Sir, never again. Thank you for our school and the students who will be able to come here."

The professor called his brother at the Village Bank. "Brother, guess what? Governor Turnmiester is giving our Genoris University five million dollars."

There was a pause, and his brother spoke. "I know. I

had talked with the governor and sent him this gold nugget I had in my safe. I can't believe that gold nugget was worth five million dollars."

The professor, shaking his head and smiling, in tears, said, "Thank you, Brother. I love you, Brother."

Darnell was leading the police and Mr. Morcort into the warm tunnel, walking down the rock steps toward the Great Fountain. Darnell motioned at the fountain. "That is gold around the fountain. We would ride the steam to get out of the cave."

The officers looked and couldn't believe what they were seeing. They passed the fountain and walked down the lighted path toward the tunnels where the cave people had lived. The police covered their noses with handkerchiefs because of the sulfur smell. They saw the platform with fire on both sides leading to the room entrance where King Daggerdash had lived.

Roscoe, with Chief Boyd, Coley, and two police officers, were hanging on to Roscoe's wings. All were soaked from Roscoe diving under the water to swim under the cave wall. Roscoe would swim against the current and then would fly.

Tibby, Teboy, and Starber, with Rocklene holding Fogel's hand, sat on the ledge. They waited and waited for Roscoe. Tibby whispered to Teboy, "We haven't seen or heard any more wing-beings. Should I call Roscoe now?"

Teboy nodded to agree. Tibby started the screeching noise, calling Roscoe.

Roscoe was above the water, flying around a curve, when he heard an echo that sounded like his screeching noise. He flew down in the water, and fighting against the current, he screeched and shouted, "Coley, Tibby is calling me!"

Coley, looking at Chief Boyd and the two police officers riding Roscoe, shouted, "We have found Tibby, Fogel, Teboy, and Starber. Roscoe, please go and find them and bring them back to us now."

Roscoe screeched and gently dropped Chief Boyd, the officers, and Coley on a rock ledge above the water. Roscoe then dove under the water and swam away.

Tibby continued his screeching, and Starber barked.

Fogel shouted, "Tib, there is the wave and Roscoe."

Roscoe screeched, slapped the water with his wings, hard, and shouted, "Tibby, Fogel, Teboy, and Starber, are you ready to go on to Tura Land? I left Coley with the police on a ledge when I heard Tibby calling me."

Tibby was beside himself, and Fogel couldn't believe what he had heard. Starber was barking, and Teboy spoke. "We can't leave Coley and the police on a ledge; the hide-beings might find them."

Fogel snickered. "Teboy, Tib, that's okay. The police have guns."

Teboy, concerned, shouted, "What is a gun?"

Tibby shouted, "Roscoe, you have to take us to Coley and the police!"

Roscoe screeched, slapped his wing in the water, and hollered, "Hang on to my wing."

Rocklene, holding Fogel's hand, shouted, "On, on, on, esaelp, Fogel, t'nod evael em!" (No, no, no, please, Fogel, don't leave me!)

Fogel replied, "Rocklene, Uoy evah ot nruter ot ruoy ylimaf." (You have to return to your family.) "Si evah ot nruter ot ym ylimaf." (I have to return to my family.)

Teboy grabbed Rocklene, still trying to hold Fogel's

hand, asking, "Tibby, Fogel, Starber, can you wait here while Roscoe carries Rocklene and Teboy to Tura Land?"

Tibby, holding Starber, started walking with Teboy and Rocklene toward Roscoe.

Fogel shouted, "Tib, please don't go. You and Starber stay with me, please."

Roscoe screeched and slapped his wing in the water, hollering, "Tibby, Fogel, Starber, stay here. Roscoe take Teboy and Rocklene to Tura Land. Roscoe will return, taking Tibby, Fogel, Starber to the cave lake!"

Chief Boyd and the two officers were looking around and started to climb the rock ledges. Coley spoke. "Please don't go anywhere. You might be hurt. The cave is dangerous. The animals in the cave are dangerous."

Chief Boyd asked, "What kind of animals live in this cave?"

Coley replied, "The hide-being will eat you. They look like a big bear. A furry rat no-sees-um will bite you. The wing-beings will take you to their nests and eat you. We lived with the cave people. They would trap a hide-being. kill it, eat it, and use the hide for their bodies. There are many hide-beings and wing-beings in the cave."

Chief Boyd sat down and motioned for his officers to sit with him.

❋

Governor Turnmiester asked his secretary to call the mayor. "Mr. Mayor Jobber, this is Governor Turnmiester calling you from his state capital office. Please hold, and I will connect you."

There was a pause, and Governor Turnmiester spoke. "Mayor Jobber, it seems a lot of excitement is happing in and around your village. I have decided to come visit you. I have been hearing all kinds of stories from my staff about gold in your creek. I will fly over there early this afternoon. I will plan to see you about four o'clock at your office. By the way, could you have a Mr. Brent Quizzley who owns the Village Bank at your office so I can talk with him and personally thank him for his donation of a gold nugget to our Genoris University?"

Mayor Jobber replied, "I will be here with Mr. Brent Quizzley and our Village Police Chief Boyd."

❋

Mayor Jobber, short, heavy, wearing glasses, and partially bald, called the Village Police Department.

"Village Police Department, can I help you?"

"This is Mayor Jobber, and I want to talk to Chief Boyd."

"I will connect you to his office. Hold on, please."

"Hello, this is Sergeant Jill."

"This is Mayor Jobber, and I want to talk with Chief Boyd."

Sergeant Jill advised, "The chief is not here."

Mayor Jobber paused, then asked, "Sergeant Jill, do you know where Chief Boyd is, and can I contact him or can you tell him that Governor Turnmiester will be in my office later today? I want Chief Boyd to meet our governor."

Sergeant Jill replied, "Mayor Jobber, the chief is at this time busy investigating several boys missing at the Morcorts' farm outside the village."

Mayor Jobber asked, "Is that in the location of the creek that has been found with gold? The governor is concerned about the creek after a professor lied about a volcano eruption."

Sergeant Jill replied, "Yes, I know about the incident. I will try to locate the chief. Thank you for calling us."

Tibby, Fogel, and Starber were on Roscoe, holding his

wing while swimming with the current. Coley heard the screeching and saw the boys and Starber on Roscoe.

Coley shouted, "Roscoe has the boys and Starber!" Chief Boyd and the two officers helped pull the boys up on the ledge and off Roscoe.

Roscoe screeched, slapped the water, and shouted, "Roscoe go now to Tura Land and find family!"

Coley shouted, "Roscoe, thank you for finding Tibby, Fogel, Teboy, and Starber!" Coley grabbed Tibby, planting a kiss on his cheek and saying, "Oh, Tibby, Fogel, and Starber, you are really here. I have been worried about you."

Fogel snickered and said, "Hey, Tib, you should kiss Coley."

Tibby hung his head, getting red in the face.

Coley asked, "Where is Teboy?"

Roscoe replied, "Roscoe take Teboy and Rocklene to Tura Land."

Tibby hung his head with tears flowing and asked in a quivering voice, "Roscoe, can you take me to Tura Land?"

Coley looked at Roscoe, hollering, "Roscoe, if you take Tibby to Tura Land, you are no longer my friend!"

Roscoe screeched and slapped the water with his wing. "Sorry, Tibby, but Coley and Darnell have been my friends. I can't take you to Tura Land, where I left Teboy and Rocklene."

Coley grabbed Tibby's hand and whispered, "Please, Tibby, forget about Elock. I don't want you to get hurt. Who is Rocklene? Tibby, who is Rocklene?"

Tibby smiled, and Starber jumped on Fogel, barking. Tibby replied, "Coley, ask Fogel about Rocklene."

Chief Boyd asked, "Roscoe, can you take us all back to the cave lake?"

Roscoe replied, "I will try. The flowing water will help. All hop on Roscoe now."

They sat down on Roscoe, and Chief Boyd said, "We are glad you boys are here with us and safe. Now we need to get back to the cave lake and the stairs taking us to the barn." Looking at the two officers, Chief Boyd demanded, "People, you have heard and seen what no one will believe. You never tell anyone what you have heard or seen. Do you understand?"

The officers nodded their heads as Roscoe shouted, "Hang on; Roscoe swim under cave wall now."

They were back in the cave lake. Roscoe swam close to the ledge by the stairs.

They jumped from Roscoe onto the rock ledge. Roscoe

screeched, slapped the water, and shouted, "Roscoe go to Tura Land and find family."

There was a splash, and Roscoe disappeared. Coley, holding Tibby's hand, asked, "Tibby, do you believe we will ever see Roscoe again?"

Tibby didn't answer, and Starber was whining.

Darnell hollered, "Dad, there's Coley, Tibby, Fogel, Starber, and the police!"

Chief Boyd waited until all were together and started talking about their adventures in the cave. Coley attempted to hold Tibby's hand, but Tibby, still disappointed about Coley telling Roscoe not to take him to Tura Land, moved his hand away from her.

Governor Turnmiester was tall, had medium build, and wore a blue suit and blue shirt with no tie. He was now in Mayor Jobber's office with Brent Quizzley, the owner of the Village Bank. They were waiting for Chief Boyd. Sergeant Jill arrived with two officers.

Mayor Jobber asked, "Sergeant, where is the chief?" Several newspeople were standing close to Governor Turnmiester, taking pictures.

Sergeant Jill replied, "The chief is still out of the office, and we haven't been able to contact him."

Governor Turnmiester walked over to Brent Quizzley, praising him for his donation to Genoris University. The governor began asking questions. "Mr. Quizzley, where in this world did you find that gold nugget?"

Brent Quizzley replied, "The gold nugget was given to me to pay the village paperboy each week with a nice tip by mail for a Mr. Morcort. However, the paper was stopped recently by the Morcorts living on the farm, so I sent the gold nugget to you. Governor Turnmiester, thank you for using the gold nugget for a grant."

Governor Turnmiester said, "There is so much conversation about gold in the village creek. Did Mr. Morcort get the gold nugget from the creek?"

Brent Quizzley shook his head and replied, "Sir, Mr. Morcort never told me where he found the gold nugget."

Governor Turnmiester, looking at all the people, police, and newspeople, announced, "I would like to see this creek where people are looking for gold and pay a visit to the Morcorts' home."

A VISIT

Tibby. Fogel, Coley, and Starber, with Chief Boyd, his police officers, Darnell, and Mr. Morcort, climbed the stairs to the barn. Governor Turnmiester and Mayor Jobber, with the Village Police and newspeople, were watching the people in the creek looking for gold. The newspeople were taking pictures.

The group walked up the path to the Morcorts' farmhouse. Governor Turnmiester knocked on the front door. The door opened, and Mrs. Morcort was amazed looking at all the people. The newspeople started asking her questions.

The governor, asking her questions, waved his hands, saying, "Is this the Morcorts'?"

Mrs. Morcort nodded yes and shut the door.

The governor looked at Mayor Jobbers and whispered, "I don't believe she knows who we are." The governor knocked on the door, but there was no answer.

Several newspeople were looking around and went in the barn. They saw the open floor door and the stairs. They were taking pictures, and several started walking down the steps.

The police, Mr. Morcort, Tibby, Fogel, Starber, Coley, and Darnell were talking and walking up the stairs as they met the newspeople. Mr. Morcort said, "You are trespassing on my property and must leave now."

Darnell hollered, "You people are trespassing on our property!"

Chief Boyd spoke. "Please follow us up the stairs! We can answer your questions in the barn!"

Arriving in the barn, the newspeople started asking questions. Darnell started to talk, but a police officer grabbed Darnell, saying, "We received a complaint about an animal in the storage shelter below us. We found several rats, and Mr. Morcort is going to call the exterminators."

Mr. Morcort shook his head, saying, "Yes, we have a rat

problem." Mr. Morcort closed the barn floor door, thanking the officers with them. Mr. Morcort walked from the barn and saw many people standing in front of his house. Some were taking pictures. He spotted Sergeant Jill and asked, "Why are all these people here?"

Sergeant Jill replied, "Mr. Morcort, it's the governor and the mayor with newspeople. Have you seen Chief Boyd?" Sergeant Jill smiled. "I see the chief now." She approached Chief Boyd and saw Tibby, Fogel, Starber, and the Morcorts with the other police officers. She asked, "Sir, where is their son Teboy?"

Chief Boyd cleared his throat and replied, "The Morcorts' son Teboy is still under the barn. Mr. Morcort told me we will let Teboy stay there until dark."

Sergeant Jill whispered, "Governor Turnmiester and Mayor Jobber are wanting information about the gold in the creek."

Mr. Morcort whispered, "Chief Boyd, is this going to create a serious trespassing problem for us?"

The chief nodded his head, whispering, "You get a fence and No Trespassing signs."

Mr. Morcort watched as the governor, mayor, and newspeople were walking down to the creek, talking to people panning for gold. Mr. Morcort grabbed Darnell and entered their house. Tibby, Fogel, and Starber were about to leave on their bikes when Coley shouted at them. "Tibby, Fogel, Starber, come here, hurry!"

Tibby and Fogel dropped their bikes and ran toward Coley.

Tibby asked, "What's going on, Coley?"

Coley, smiling and looking at both boys and Starber, whispered, "Follow me back in the barn." They arrived and Coley opened the floor door and they could hear screeching and more screeching. They walked down the steps leading to the cave.

Coley whispered, "Roscoe is making that noise and has to be in the cave lake." They arrived at the bottom of the stairs, and there was more loud screeching and huge waves and more screeching and slapping the water. Roscoe spoke.

"Coley, Tibby, Fogel, and Starber, I have brought my family here from Tura Land. The cave people are no longer here, so we can live here. Teboy and Rocklene are back with their families at Tura Land. The cave people were happy to see Teboy and Rocklene. The cave people arriving at Tura Land were trying to catch my family with nets. Thank you for showing me how to go to Tura Land. I and my family will remain here in the cave lake and creek. Please come see us often and ride us, or we will miss you." There was more loud screeching and splashing in the water by Roscoe and his family.

Fogel, laughing, said, "Coley, you and Darnell will have Roscoe and his family here. You will have to teach our English language to Roscoe's family. Can Tib, Rex, Kurpit, Jerk, Mouse, Starber, and I come here to swim and ride Roscoe and his family?"

More screeching, and Roscoe replied, "Tibby, Fogel, Starber, Coley, and Darnell, we want to be your friends. True friends together, always."

Tibby moaned and asked, "Roscoe, will you take me to Tura Land so I can find Elock?"

Roscoe screeched and splashed the water, and Coley shouted, "Roscoe, no, please, never take Tibby to Tura Land if you want to stay my friend."

Fogel shouted, "Come on, Tib. I ain't afraid of wing-beings, the hide-beings, and the no-sees-um."

Coley shouted, "No, Fogel, you and Tibby can't go to Tura Land!"

Tibby looked at Fogel and Starber, shaking his head, with tears flowing, and replied, "Coley is right. I want to find Elock, but it's too dangerous."

They waved at Roscoe and walked up the stairs to the

barn. Coley closed the floor door, walking with them to the bridge and their bikes.

Coley continued speaking. "Tibby, I am sorry I stopped you from going to Tura Land. Please forgive me." Coley grabbed Tibby, pleading, "Tibby, please don't be mad at me. I don't want you to get hurt by the cave people. King Daggerdash does not like earthlings. He might hurt you, Fogel, and Starber. He kept us in the cave for years before you, Fogel, Starber, and Roscoe rescued us. I don't want that to happen to you, Fogel, and Starber."

Tibby, with tears in his eyes, whispered, "Coley, I know you're right. We understand, don't we, Fogel and Starber?" Starber jumped on Coley, whining. Fogel raised his hand, motioning for Coley and Tibby. They chanted, "True friends together, always."

Monday morning Kurpit, Jer, and Mac were at the tree house. Kurpit, seeing Starber sitting by the tree, walked up to him and petted him.

Kurpit climbed the ladder on the walnut tree, about to knock on the door, when it opened, with Fogel looking at him.

Fogel spoke. "You have mud on the walls to clean off

inside our tree house. Soon as you finish, you will belong here as members. By the garage is a bucket with rags to clean this mud. Get going before I put bumps on your heads."

Tibby was leaning back against the tree house wall, watching Kurpit, Jer, and Mac cleaning the mud mess. The job was completed, and Rex thanked them, welcoming them as members to the tree house. They all raised their hands together, chanting. "True friends together, always."

Tibby whispered to Rex, "What a summer. I never did find Elock."

Rex replied, "TB, you got to be kidding me."

Fogel, smiling, said, "Tib, I am so glad that you, Starber, and Rex allowed me to become your friend. Boy, what a summer. Talk about adventure, excitement, and surprises."

"We have done it. We are now friends," Kurpit said. "Tibby, Fogel, Rex, thanks to you guys, Starber, Coley, and Darnell, we are now friends." Kurpit looked at Jer and Mac. "Ain't that right, Jerk and Mouse?" Jer and Mac nodded.

Fogel, laughing, reported, "Tib and guys, we have our tree house. We have a cave with a lake where we now can swim and ride Roscoe and his family with Coley and Darnell Morcort."

Tibby hung his head, then smiled. "Fogel, do you miss Rocklene?"

Fogel replied, "Tib, do you miss Coley?" Both boys rolled on the floor, laughing. Starber jumped at the tree, barking.

A GREAT
SURPRISE

Kurpit asked, "Hey, Tibby, Fogel, what's this about a Rocklene and Coley?"

Fogel replied, "It's a joke between Tib and I. We joke often, right, Tib?"

Tibby nodded. He sat back in the corner of the tree house against the wall, thinking about this past summer and how he never did find Elock. Coley had stopped him from riding Roscoe to Tura Land. She was right because it was too dangerous with the wing-beings, hide-beings, and the no-sees-um rats. He moaned, "No Elock but a great summer with the Morcorts, Fogel, Rex, Starber, and now Kurpit, Jerk, and Mouse."

Fogel jumped up, and the tree house creaked and moved. "Hey, guys, let's go to Coley's and ride Roscoe and his family in the cave lake. You guys agree?"

Kurpit nodded, remembering his experience with Roscoe. Jer and Mouse chimed in. "Let's go."

The boys were back on their bikes riding to the bridge with Starber running in front. There were numerous cars and small pickup trucks on the bridge. A sign was posted at the bridge front. THIS IS THE VILLAGE CREEK, AND YOU ARE REQUIRED TO REPORT ANY GOLD FOUND TO THE VILLAGE MAYOR'S OFFICE UNDER PENALTY OF THE VILLAGE LAW.

Fogel was laughing and whispered to Tibby, "Boy, Tib, if they only knew what we know. Can you imagine what the mayor would do?"

Starber barked, and Tibby shook his head, replying, "We aren't here to pan for gold."

Rex read the sign and whispered, "You got to be kidding me." The boys continued up the lane to the Morcorts' farm.

Darnell was playing with his toys on the porch when he saw Starber and the boys on bikes. He ran into the house, hollering, "Coley, your boyfriend, Tibby, is here."

Coley opened the door, and little TJ ran to Starber. Fogel said, "Hey, Coley, can we get in the cave lake to ride Roscoe and his family?"

Coley walked over to Tibby and looked at him, replying, "Tibby, you promise me you won't ask Roscoe to take you to Tura Land."

Tibby nodded, gritted his teeth, and whispered, "Coley, I promise." Coley opened the front door, hollering for her dad.

Mr. Morcort walked by Coley, looking at the boys and asking, "What is the problem, boys?"

Fogel approached Mr. Morcort and announced, "We came over here to see Coley and Darnell and ride Roscoe in the cave lake."

Mr. Morcort noticed the vehicles on the bridge and people in the creek panning for gold. He asked, "You boys haven't told anyone about our secret, have you?"

Fogel replied, "Sir, no one here will ever tell anyone. If they do I will place bumps on their heads."

Mr. Morcort, grinning, said, "Fogel, I bet you would do just that." Darnell hollered, "We want to ride Roscoe in the cave lake. Please, Dad, can we?"

Mr. Morcort smiled. "Okay, you kids stay together with Roscoe and his family in the cave lake. We will go down together."

The barn floor door was open, and the group started walking down the steps. They arrived in the cave and could see the waterfall and the various color sprays. Coley started screeching to call Roscoe. The group waited, sitting on the rock ledge.

Darnell shouted, "I will call Roscoe under the water." He took off his shoes and jumped in the lake, swimming underwater and screeching. The group waited, and Darnell surfaced. There was no Roscoe or his family. Kurpit asked, "Fogel, can we jump off the ledges into the lake?"

Mr. Morcort broke the silence with an order. "Roscoe and his family are not here, so let's all leave." He motioned for the group to follow him up the steps. Kurpit helped Mr. Morcort close the floor door. They looked around, but Tibby, Fogel, and Starber were missing.

Coley was shouting, with tears in her eyes. "Dad, Tibby, Fogel, and Starber are still in the cave."

Mr. Morcort replied, "Are you sure? Darnell, look outside the barn to see if the boys are there."

Darnell ran outside looking around and returned to the

group, replying, "Dad, they're not outside."

Mr. Morcort opened the floor door and was angry. "I'll walk down the stairs with Coley and Darnell." Looking at Kurpit, Jer, and Mac, he said, "You boys stay here. Come on, Coley and Darnell." Mr. Morcort, Coley, and Darnell were walking down the path toward the Great Fountain when they saw a bright light with various colors disappear. Mr. Morcort asked, "Kids, did you see that bright light that disappeared?"

Darnell shouted, "Dad, Coley, the guys and Starber are riding on the Great Fountain steam to leave the cave!"

Coley asked, "Darnell, are you sure?"

Darnell replied, "Coley, we have ridden on the steam to get out of the cave several times. Dad, can we go back to the cave lake so we can ride Roscoe and his family? Tibby, Fogel, and Starber will come down the stairs from the barn with their friends." Mr. Morcort motioned for Coley and Darnell to follow him.

They arrived at the cave lake, but Tibby, Fogel, Starber, and their friends were not there. Coley heard a screeching noise.

Darnell hollered, "Dad, Coley, it's Roscoe and his family!"

Coley started up the steps, turned around, and shouted, "Dad I am going to see if Tibby, Fogel, and Starber are in the barn with their friends!"

Darnell shouted, "I get to ride on Roscoe!"

Coley arrived in the barn, finding Kurpit, Jer, and Mac sitting on the floor. She asked, "Have you guys seen Tibby, Fogel, and Starber?"

Kurpit replied, "They haven't been here."

Coley could hear the screeching below and asked, "Do you still want to ride Roscoe and his family in the cave lake?"

The boys together shouted, "Yes!"

Coley approached her dad, who was sitting on a rock ledge, watching the boys riding Roscoe and his family. Coley, with tears in her eyes, hugged her dad, asking, "Dad, why aren't Tibby, Fogel, and Starber here? When they left the cave, they would come back in the barn to be with their friends, wouldn't they?"

Mr. Morcort shook his head, replying, "Coley, Tibby, Fogel, and Starber aren't here. They might be down at the creek watching people or maybe fishing. Go and have fun with your friends riding Roscoe and his family."

❄

Tibby had grabbed Fogel as the group started walking up the steps from the cave to the barn and whispered, "Fogel, let's you, me, and Starber ride out of the cave on the steam from the Great Fountain." Fogel turned around, and the boys, with Starber, ran to the tunnel. They were standing by the Great Fountain, waiting for the steam to jump into for a ride out of the cave.

There was a huge flash of lights in various colors. Fogel jumped back, and Tibby couldn't believe what he was seeing. Starber started growling, then whining. Down below the Great Fountain on the path was a funny-shaped machine that looked like a brown bean. The machine doors opened, and there was Teboy, still dressed in his earthling shirt, walking toward Tibby and Fogel. Starber ran to greet Teboy, jumping on him. Someone was walking behind Teboy.

Tibby and Fogel were about to run when Tibby heard a voice in his head. "Tibby, don't be scared when you see me. I am with Teboy."

Tibby hollered, "Fogel, did somebody talk to you in your head?"

Fogel heard the same voice. "Fogel, don't be scared. I am with Teboy." Starber was whining and jumping on the someone.

Teboy spoke. "Tibby, Fogel, Starber, I have found Elock and told him about all of you. King Daggerdash has ordered us to find you boys and Starber since you saved me and Rocklene, his niece. We were going to use the no-sees-um and ride on the steam inside the Great Fountain to leave this cave to find you."

The boys could now see Elock. He was not human looking but different. His head was big with large glowing eyes, and he had no ears, was wearing a brown uniform, and had small wings attached to his back.

Tibby was laughing, jumping up and down, shouting, "Fogel, I told you Elock in my dream could be real! He looks like the Elock in my dream! That brown machine looks like the machine in my dream!"

Teboy spoke. "This is Elock, who our cave people have talked about. When Roscoe took Rocklene and I to Tura Land to our parents, the cave people and King Daggerdash were thrilled to see us. I told our king how you found Rocklene and I, bringing us to Tura Land."

Tibby whispered, "Teboy, you were with us when we found Rocklene."

Teboy whispered, "I know, but my story made King Daggerdash happy. He told me that I could ask him for anything, and it would be granted. I asked the king if he knew Elock. He told me about Elock and took me to him. King Daggerdash asked us to find you, Fogel, and Starber. We are to bring you to Tura Land so the king, our parents, and the cave people can thank you."

Starber was licking Elock's face while Elock was petting him. Elock stood, and Tibby, Fogel, and Teboy heard in their heads, "Please follow me to my home machine."

Tibby, holding Starber, followed Fogel, Teboy, and Elock. The machine doors opened, and they stood in the machine resembling a brown bean. Elock was sitting in front of them and touching different screens on several computers. Several minutes passed, and the machine doors opened. There stood Rocklene, holding King Daggerdash's hand.

Rocklene jumped up and down, shouting, "Fogel, Fogel, s'ti em, Rocklene!" (Fogel, Fogel, it's me, Rocklene!)

The cave people surrounded the machine and chanted, "Tibby, Fogel, Starber, knaht uoy rof gnivas Teboy dna Rocklene." (Tibby, Fogel, Starber, thank you for saving Teboy and Rocklene.)

Rocklene grabbed Fogel's hand and kissed him on the cheek. Fogel hung his head, embarrassed, and Tibby smiled. Starber was licking the faces of the children who were petting him. The king's son and the cave people, were acting excited, jumping up and down chanting, "Tibby, Fogel, Starber, ruo seoreh." (Tibby, Fogel, Starber, our heroes.) King Daggerdash motioned for Elock, Teboy, Tibby, Fogel, Rocklene, and Starber, who was whining, to follow him. The cave was huge, with a larger cave lake and a waterfall flowing with various color sprays. Above on several rock ledges trees and flowers were growing.

Plants were growing from open areas that looked like gardens. Tibby and Fogel had a hard time believing what they were seeing. It was amazing, as sunlight was shining through the cave ceiling. Tibby and Fogel, with Rocklene holding his hand, continued looking at Tura Land. They followed King Daggerdash and the cave people to another rock ledge. In the center of the ledge was a leaping fire with an animal carcass roasting on a metal rotating spear. Guards wearing swords and holding spears surrounded the fire. They saw their king and bowed.

King Daggerdash spoke. "Ym elpoep, ew era ereh rehtegot ot yas knaht uoy ot Tibby, Fogel, dna Starber rof gniucser ruo Rocklene dna Teboy." (My people, we are here together to say thank you to Tibby, Fogel, and Starber for rescuing our Rocklene and Teboy.) The king shouted, "Sdraug, gnirb ot em detsaor hide-being rof ruo sdneirf!" (Guards, bring to me roasted hide-being for our friends!)

"Knaht uoy." (Thank you.) "Yojne hide-being." (Enjoy hide-being.)

The guards placed a huge hunk of hide-being on a large leaf for Teboy, Rocklene, Fogel, Tibby, and Starber, who were sitting on the cave floor. King Daggerdash sat on the cave floor by his leaf filled with hide-being. He motioned for all the cave people to join him. The cave people chanted, "Sey, taerg eno." (Yes, Great One.) The guards were cutting meat from the hide-being and throwing pieces to the cave people.

Fogel said, "Hey, Tib, we are eating a hide-being, who would eat us."

Tibby looked at Elock, thinking, "Elock, can you hear my thoughts?"

Tibby heard in his head Elock's reply. "Tibby, I hear you."

Tibby, thinking, began asking questions. "Elock, do you live in the cave with the cave people?"

Elock replied, "I am living here now, but I come from a different world, a planet like yours but larger than your earth. Your home, the cave people tell me, is called earth. My home is called Winggots. My home is far from your earth. I was traveling in my circle ship and crashed into your earth's huge water. My ship sank and was carried over the waterfalls into this cave lake. The king's son was living here with his mother, who died, going to their great spirit. I gave him toys when he left here with guards to be with his father, the king."

Tibby was so excited and couldn't believe he was sitting beside Elock, who was in his dream and living in the cave. Tibby heard in his head Elock asking, "Tibby, what is a dream?"

Tibby thinking, replied, "Humans on earth have to sleep. Sleep is where you rest for several hours. While I slept I was seeing you and your home machine in what we call a dream." Tibby was thinking how Coley had warned him about King Daggerdash and the cave people being dangerous people. Tibby was grinning and thinking that if only Coley could be there and see him with the cave people and Elock.

Tibby heard in his head Elock asking, "Tibby, who is Coley?"

Before Tibby could answer, King Daggerdash stood up and spoke. "Ym elpoep, ruo Rocklene sah deksa ruoy taerg eno ot evah Fogel, ruo dneirf, ot niamer ereh dna evil htiw su." (My people, our Rocklene has asked your great one to have Fogel, our friend, to remain here and live with us.)

Fogel dropped the hide-being bone he was chewing on,

tapping Tibby and whispering, "Tib, we have to leave here now."

Rocklene grabbed Fogel's hand, smiling and looking at him.

Tibby, thinking, spoke to Elock. "Elock, can you take us to see your circle ship? Then take us to the Great Fountain, where you found us?"

In his head Tibby heard Elock reply, "Tibby, I will ask the king if you, Fogel, Teboy, and Starber can go with me to see my circle ship."

Tibby waited and watched when King Daggerdash nodded and said, "Tibby, Fogel, Starber, dna Teboy tnaw ot evael ot ees Elock's pihs." (Tibby, Fogel, Starber, and Teboy want to leave to see Elock's ship.)

Rocklene shouted, "Nac Si og htiw Fogel?" (Can I go with Fogel?)

Teboy, standing, shouted, "Taerg Gnik Daggerdash, Si lliw og." (Great King Daggerdash, I will go.) "Si lliw gnirb kcab Rocklene dna Fogel ot evil ereh." (I will bring back Rocklene and Fogel to live here.)

Tibby tapped Fogel, whispering, "We have to follow Elock to his machine." Starber was whining, and Tibby picked Starber up, holding him. Rocklene, holding Fogel's hand, and Teboy walked behind Elock.

Teboy was thinking, "Elock, take Tibby, Fogel, Starber, and me to the Great Fountain now." The machine doors opened. Once again all were standing, and Elock was sitting and touching the screens on the computers. The machine doors opened, and Teboy was holding Rocklene, who let go of Fogel's hand to holler, cry, and try to kick Teboy. She was shouting, "Fogel, Fogel, t'nod og!" (Fogel, Fogel, don't go!)

Tibby, Fogel, Starber, and Teboy jumped from the machine as the doors closed. There was a brilliant light, and the machine disappeared. The boys raced to the Great Fountain and, hearing the steam, jumped and soon were outside the cave.

Standing above the opening, the three boys looked at each other, and Starber was barking. Fogel said, "Thanks, Teboy, for helping us. Are you going back in the cave to live with your people?"

Teboy shook his head, replying, "Teboy not go back to people. King Daggerdash will be angry with Teboy and dangerous. Teboy not bring Fogel with Rocklene back to cave people when Elock returns Rocklene to cave people. King be angry with Teboy. Teboy now live with Darnell Morcort."

The boys walked down the rock ledges, following

Starber back to their camp. They dropped the tent, and Fogel carried it to their bikes on the bridge. They watched as Teboy surprised Darnell, who was playing with toys on the farmhouse porch. Darnell jumped up, hugging Teboy and hollering, "Dad, Mom, Coley, Teboy is here!"

Tibby and Fogel, with Starber running ahead, rode their bikes back to the village.

Fogel had tied the tent to his back. Riding close to Tibby, he asked, "Hey, Tib, are we going to tell anyone about our latest adventure?"

Tibby replied, "We tell Rex and no one else, agreed?"

The boys dropped their bikes in Rex's backyard and climbed the walnut tree ladder. Rex looked out his window and saw Tibby, Fogel, and Starber. Rex left the house, climbed the tree ladder, and tapped their secret code on the tree house door.

The door opened, and Rex was with Tibby and Fogel, and Starber had found his favorite spot by the tree. Tibby and Fogel told Rex about their latest adventure, and all Rex could say was, "TB, Fogel, you got to be kidding me."

The boys raised their hands and chanted, "True friends together, always."

Tibby whispered, "Rex, you can't tell anyone about our adventure."

Rex, looking at Tibby and Fogel, shook his head, replying, "TB, Fogel, give me your hands."

The boys raised their hands together, chanting, "True friends together, always." Starber was jumping at the tree and barking.

ABOUT THE AUTHOR

Starber was Tibby's best friend. Above is the author and his best friend, Kim, a United States trained Army sentry dog. Carl Kegerreis was drafted into the United States Army and graduated from the Army Fort Knox Military Police Training School in March 1962.

Kim and Carl Kegerreis trained at the United States Lackland Air Force Base Sentry Dog School in San Antonio, Texas, and were transferred to the Army Nike

Missile Base in Dillsboro, Indiana, protecting the missiles underground on tripods during the Cold War with the Soviet Union.

Carl Kegerreis worked on the CSX Transportation Railroad for thirty-three years, retiring in 1999 after becoming the division's chief of police. He lives in Ohio with his wife of fifty-five years and has three children and five grandchildren.

CPSIA information can be obtained
at www.ICGtesting.com
Printed in the USA
LVHW090457090519
617222LV00001B/61/P